"I'm on your side,

How desperately she wanted to believe it. "If you were on my side, you wouldn't have kissed me," she bit out, avoiding his gaze. He had no idea how deep her feelings went. She hated that everything had changed, that he wasn't the person she thought he was.

"I tried hard not to," Caige said in a husky voice. His nearness was too much.

"You didn't try hard enough. That was really taking unfair advantage."

"I know, but if you were a man and could have seen how beautiful you looked in the glow of the Christmas tree lights, you would understand."

Dear Reader,

Years ago, a boy in my neighborhood was hit by a car in front of his home. The setting sun had gotten in the driver's eyes and blinded him. It only took one second to leave the boy brain injured. I remember how the tragedy altered the lives of his family members.

Our neighborhood was called on to help. Dozens of people, including myself, went to their home to work with the boy. We were taught how to give him psychomotor patterning to keep his muscles moving. Since that time, science has concluded that it probably didn't help. But I know that all of us coming to the house to do our part let that family know we cared. Furthermore, I realized it could have been my child. I know I would have wanted and needed all the support possible from those around me.

In my novel, Caige Dawson adores his precious boy and will do anything for him. With tears in my eyes and heart, I dedicate this book to all devoted parents like him, doing angels' work.

Enjoy.

Rebecca Winters

A Texas Ranger's Christmas

REBECCA WINTERS

TORONTO NEW YORK LONDON
AMSTERDAM PARIS SYDNEY HAMBURG
STOCKHOLM ATHENS TOKYO MILAN MADRID
PRAGUE WARSAW BUDAPEST AUCKLAND

ISBN-13: 978-0-373-75381-9

A TEXAS RANGER'S CHRISTMAS

ABOUT THE AUTHOR

Rebecca Winters, whose family of four children has now swelled to include five beautiful grandchildren, lives in Salt Lake City, Utah, in the land of the Rocky Mountains. With canyons and high alpine meadows full of wildflowers, she never runs out of places to explore. They, plus her favorite vacation spots in Europe, often end up as backgrounds for her romance novels, because writing is her passion, along with her family and church. Rebecca loves to hear from readers. If you wish to email her, please visit her website at www.cleanromances.com.

Books by Rebecca Winters

Who doesn't recall the line, "I think that I shall never see, a poem as lovely as a tree"?
Since writing this novel, I have a new appreciation for them thanks to Jim Houser, Regional Forest Health Coordinator at the Texas Forest Service, to whom I dedicate this book. Besides his invaluable contribution, I'm especially grateful for his patience and willingness to teach me about trees when he has so many other calls on his time.

Chapter One

"Hey, buddy—we're here now. Let's go inside."

Texas Ranger Caige Dawson unfastened his son's seat belt so he could get out of the car. Even at eight years old, it was clear Josh was going to be tall like Caige. On cue, his boy started to cry and hugged him for dear life before clutching his hand.

Since the accident three years ago, which had turned the Dawson family inside out and resulted in divorce, Caige went through this ritual with Josh anytime they had to be separated. Usually a special school bus picked him up and brought him home, but an incident on the bus last month had scared him and he didn't want to ride it or go to school anymore.

For the past few weeks Caige had been working closely with Josh. He'd gotten him to the point where Josh didn't have to be carried inside the school to his classroom in order to get him to stay. Lately he'd made it through a whole school day and had accepted driving home with Elly, Caige's housekeeper and Josh's caregiver, in her car. This was an encouraging sign according to Dr. Sweeney, the neuropsychologist, who said that pretty soon they'd reintroduce him to the bus.

Caige opened the school door. "Everyone's going in."

Josh's tear-filled blue eyes, light in color like his mother's, fastened on his father in panic. This was the moment when Caige had to harden himself against that look. It begged his dad to take him back home.

"See? There's Mrs. Wright."

The special-education teacher smiled. "Come on in, Josh. We've been waiting for you." She gave Josh a warm hug that, Caige noted thankfully, was reciprocated before she led him to his desk. Caige turned away quickly and headed out of the school to the parking lot.

He decided some angels came to earth disguised as people. Mrs. Wright was one of them. Now wasn't the time to worry that this was her last year of teaching, or whether Elly would tell him she'd made up her mind to move to Lubbock so she could be near her daughter and grandchildren. Caige had a good system going with Elly. To change anything in the routine would cause a major earthquake for his son.

Although Elly hadn't said anything specific, she would probably make the decision any day now. Her daughter and son-in-law were begging her to spend Christmas with them while they found a place for her to live that was close by.

Christmas…only three weeks away. Caige had been contemplating getting Josh a dog. He'd discussed it with Dr. Sweeney. A dog would provide stimulation and love, but would take a team effort to train. Until he knew Elly's plans, he couldn't think of adding a pet to their household.

As for Josh's mother, he had no idea if Liz would

make an appearance. Last Christmas had turned into a nightmare. She'd come to spend part of the day with Josh, but she was still in denial about his brain injury. It was a struggle for her to face him.

Caige had seen the horror in her eyes as she regarded her special-needs son. Josh had to have seen it, too. He was an intelligent boy who clung to his father the whole time. When Liz left before the day was out, Caige was secretly relieved.

Liz never seemed to notice their son had been making progress. The moment he exhibited any kind of atypical behavior, it frightened her, and she fell apart.

Since the afternoon three years ago when Josh had been hit by a car in front of their house, Caige had been forced to slow down and take life a second at a time. He'd graduated to minutes, and later, hours at a time.

Liz was convinced Caige blamed her because she'd been in the house and hadn't realized their five-year-old had tried crossing the street. Nothing could have been further from the truth in his mind. Accidents happened. But he couldn't talk her out of her guilt.

If anything, he blamed himself. Their marriage had already been going through some rough stages because of his unconventional work schedule. Sometimes he had to be away for several weeks on a case. This put a heavy load on Liz.

Obviously it had been more than she could handle. When she realized Josh would never be the same again, her breakdown had been so severe, she'd moved in with her parents and filed for divorce. At the precarious moment when Josh needed both parents more than ever, Liz wasn't emotionally or physically available.

In February of this past year she'd married a divorced businessman from Austin who kept nine-to-five hours. Her visits to see their son had grown fewer and further apart. Little by little Caige was losing hope that she would ever come to accept Josh's condition and show him the love he needed from his mom.

And now, Caige was thankful he'd gotten to the point at work where he could breathe somewhat normally for the length of Josh's school day. Provided there were no incidents like an illness or another student's sudden meltdown, that is.

A few minutes later he pulled into the underground parking of headquarters in downtown Austin and took the elevator to his division's suite on the second floor. Before he reached his own office, his superior, Mac Leesom, gave him the nod to join him and another man in the conference room.

"Caige? You haven't met Agent Tim Robbins with the FBI in Fort Worth. He and I go way back."

The older man, wearing a suit and tie, shook Caige's hand. "It's a privilege, Captain Dawson. I've been wanting to meet the Ranger who headed the task force that brought in the most wanted felon in Travis County in a decade."

"Thank you. It took a massive manhunt and was a case of being in the right place at the right time to capture him."

Mac patted Caige's shoulder. His boss was close to retirement and treated Caige like one of his own sons. "Tim's here because of an unsolved case he was overseeing before he was transferred from the Austin bureau. He knows you're the best and would like you to take a look and see what you can do with it. To make this a more palatable job, he's already spoken to Judge Harkness at the third district court. He'll cooperate with you and issue warrants to help in your investigation at your request."

So this Robbins was shrewd. Caige chuckled. Harkness was the presiding judge and a tough old bird. "You're right. That's one big headache out of the way."

"Amen," Mac murmured. "I'll leave you two to talk. Buzz me if you need anything."

Caige had a stack of cases waiting on his desk, but you didn't turn Mac down when he was asking a personal favor. Once he left the room, the agent eyed Caige with a sober expression.

"This is a missing-person case. It was high-profile at the time because it was indirectly connected to the University of Texas here in Austin. Anytime something happens affecting a college student, the publicity escalates, especially when there's a beautiful woman involved. You know what I'm talking about."

Caige was afraid he did.

"Nathan Farley, a finance graduate from UT Austin, worked for the campus branch of the Yellow Rose Bank of Texas. This branch deals with a lot of student accounts. On the day in question, he finished his work, left for the day at five o'clock and was never seen again.

"His car was still parked at the bank when his wife started making phone calls. Blaire Farley, an undergraduate student at UT Austin at the time, was at home waiting for him. They lived in an apartment on East 32nd near the campus. That was five years ago, but various detectives assigned still haven't turned up anything."

Which was nothing new, Caige mused. There were dozens of missing-person cases over twenty years old now throughout Texas. Some forty, fifty, even older.

They sat down opposite each other. Agent Robbins reached in his briefcase for a file and slid it toward Caige. "Before I say more, take a look inside."

Caige opened it and scanned the first police incident report dated Wednesday, November 15. There were photographs. Some were of the then twenty-six-year-old missing man. Others showed his then twenty-four-year-old wife, Blaire. Both were dark blond and blue-eyed. Oddly enough, the good-looking pair could almost pass for brother and sister.

Married on March 14 of the same year. No children. Only married eight months.

Caige glanced through the forensics report. A double-action Ruger GP100 revolver and ammo were found on the premises of the apartment near the campus that the couple were renting at the time. It had been a gun Mr. Farley had purchased at a gun show on June 3, six months prior to his disappearance, and showed evidence of recent firing. The fingerprints on the gun matched the husband's.

The rest of the information in the file revealed exhaustive searches into morgues, hospitals and national and international DNA data banks had produced no shred of evidence that Nathan Farley was either alive or dead. Caige read through the depositions of the wife, other family members, coworkers, friends, acquaintances; in five years no one had shed any light on the man's disappearance.

He closed the file. "This is a cold case, all right."

Agent Robbins nodded. "Two days ago I received a call from the Koslovs, Blaire's parents. Her mother particularly begged me to do something to find out what happened to their son-in-law. Her family has suffered anguish."

"What about Farley's parents?"

"They're dead. His grandparents raised him here in Austin. The grandfather died when he was ten. The grandmother was well-thought-of in the neighborhood, lived on a fixed income and passed away when he turned sixteen. After that he had to make it on his own. From all I've gathered, he was an attractive, affable self-starter. The Koslovs loved him and have grieved over him.

"When they came to me, I told them I'm assigned elsewhere now, but I would see what I could do. They're devastated for their daughter, whose life might as well be over. Those are their words, not mine."

"All understandable," Caige murmured. Without a body, alive or dead, the spouse was always the first person of interest to the police. This woman, Blaire, had been that person for five years. With no family members implicated, it was a long time to be at the center of a nightmare where she would remain suspect until there was a break in the case—to prove either her innocence or her guilt.

Whether she knew where he was and wasn't telling, or had nothing to do with her husband's disappearance and had loved him—or whether she'd plotted to do away with him and had committed the perfect murder—she couldn't get divorced or married yet. She was neither fish nor fowl. Since her parents had approached the FBI again, maybe their daughter was involved with a new man and wanted closure so she could move on.

"You've met and talked with Mrs. Farley," Caige said. "What's your gut feeling about her?"

The agent shook his head. "I've been in this business too long and don't have one. We both know the most appealing person might have a criminal mind."

"Agreed."

"The Koslovs helped me bring the file up-to-date with new phone numbers and addresses. These days she goes by her maiden name, Blaire Koslov, and lives in a town house in Great Hills. At present she works for the Texas Forest Service. Here's the sheet with all the contact information, including my private number."

"Thanks."

"Let's hope a certain legendary Ranger can pull off another miracle and solve this case regardless of how it breaks. What a Christmas present it would be for that family!"

Caige lowered his head. He could wish for a miracle for all those needing one. His son, Josh, had survived the accident and was doing better than expected. That was a miracle in and of itself.

"The Koslovs are positive their son-in-law was a victim of foul play and they fervently believe in their daughter's innocence. Off the record, I'd like to believe in it, too." On that note Agent Robbins pushed himself away from the table. "Call me anytime."

"You can count on it." Caige got to his feet and shook the agent's hand.

"I'll see myself out."

After the man left, Caige moved to a side table and poured himself some coffee. He already knew how he was going to proceed, but before he did anything else, he phoned his friend and favorite source of information at police headquarters.

"Hey, Gracie."

"Caige—congratulations on nailing that lowlife! You're a hero around here. What can I do for you?"

He smiled. "I'm glad you asked. How about pulling any files of unsolved shooting crimes within Travis County between June 3 and November 15 of the year Nathan Farley disappeared."

"You *are* kidding me, right?"

"Not all of them. I only want those cases where the weapon was a double-action Ruger GP100."

"Oh. Is *that* all—"

The mother of two was fun to tease. "For now."

If any of the detectives on the case had tried to establish a link between Nathan Farley's gun and a shooting in the county between his purchase of the gun and his disappearance, Caige found no evidence of it in the file.

On the outside chance there could be a matchup of ballistics reports proving Farley had been involved in criminal activity prior to his disappearance, the case could take off in a whole new direction.

If Caige couldn't make a connection, then he'd go county by county throughout the state, checking shooting ranges from the time Farley first purchased the gun to the day he disappeared. It was entirely possible the guy was alive and living somewhere else under an assumed name. Caige would pass pictures around and hope to find out if Farley had ever done any target practice. Someone might have seen him.

"I'll be by at ten with breakfast for you, Gracie."

"Promise?"

"You can take it as a given." He hung up, needing to run his plan past Mac before he left headquarters.

WHILE BLAIRE WAITED FOR her partner, Perry, to get to the Austin office, she printed out two copies of her work sheet for the day and put one on Sheila's desk. It was getting late. Something had held him up obviously. After phoning the Drummonds to let them know she was coming, she left for her first appointment.

At ten o'clock she pulled into the Drummonds' driveway and jumped down from the cab of the white truck bearing the Texas Forest Service logo. A guy who looked around thirty, close to her age anyway, walked over to her. The sixty-three-degree weather made it a balmy December day, the kind she liked since she worked out of doors year-round.

Lighter streaks in her honey-blond hair attested to the fact that she spent a lot of her time in the sun. For practicality on the job she'd recently had it cut and layered.

"I'm Blaire Koslov, coordinator for the Austin forestry office." Since her husband's disappearance five years earlier, she'd gone by her maiden name. Because of the horrendous publicity at the time, she'd done everything possible to keep a low profile and minimize public scrutiny.

"Nice to meet you. I'm Jeremy Drummond. Sorry, but my wife waited as long as she could before she had to leave for work and couldn't be here."

"I'm sorry I was late. I waited for my colleague who usually comes on calls with me, but something has held him up. Please forgive the delay." They shook hands. "You've got a lovely stand of pecan trees around the side there."

"They're part of the reason we bought this place in the spring, but we've noticed something's wrong with several of them. I hope we didn't make a mistake purchasing this property."

"Why don't you show me the trees you're talking about first."

"Sure."

She followed him across the front yard. Before they reached them, she saw the problem immediately and called to him. "I already know what's wrong. Some of the trees have been attacked with webworm. Those unsightly webs look ugly, but it's not serious if you take care of it now. If you have a broom handy, I'll show you. Bring a box or a garbage bag, too."

His worried expression vanished. "Give me a second."

While he was gone, she walked around identifying the trees that were affected.

"Here you go."

She took the broom from him and used the handle to break open some of the webs she could reach. Being five foot six meant she wasn't short, but her height had its limitations. Still, she did her best. Soon the larvae fell out. "You want to get rid of these pests and prune any leaves that have egg masses. Since it's fall, a lot of beneficial insects have already been feeding on the eggs. Such natural predators have helped cut down on some of the problem."

He looked up. "You think I can do all this myself?"

"Probably, but you'll have to spray on a pesticide to open up those webs at the top. If you're not comfortable doing that, then call an expert who'll know the right kind of spray and let them do the job. This isn't a serious infestation. If you take care of it now, your trees will stay healthy."

A smile lit up his face. "I hope you'll forgive me when I say this, but you don't look like what you are. Whoops. That came out wrong. What I'm trying to say is, you don't expect to see such an attractive member of the forest service arrive at your door. Am I terrible to say that?"

She chuckled and started walking toward the truck. She wore hiking boots along with her green-and-khaki uniform. "Let me ask you a question before I answer. Are you a baseball player?"

"No. A tile contractor."

"Well, there you go."

His mind soon caught up with her comment and he grinned. "You actually thought I played baseball?"

"Let's just say I could imagine it. You remind me of a couple of players." He was cute.

"You're a baseball fan?"

"No. To me it's like watching paint dry." That wasn't exactly true. She used to love watching all kinds of sports, especially college football, but that was before her world had shattered. Her pleasure in just being alive had been stolen from her. Thanks to a good psychiatrist and her career, she was doing better these days.

Mr. Drummond laughed as she climbed back in the truck and shut the door. "Thank you for your expertise, Ms. Koslov."

She waved to him. "Happy to be of help."

"My wife's going to be greatly relieved. By the time she gets home, I hope to have most of those webs gone."

By the time she gets home...

Every spouse had the right to presume his or her other half would come home at the end of a busy workday. Five years ago Blaire's husband had left the bank where he worked and had never come home to their apartment for their eight-month anniversary dinner.

As Blaire backed out of the driveway and took off, she looked into the rearview mirror and saw Mr. Drummond get to work. She hoped his wife would be home on time tonight and every night for the rest of their lives. She hoped his wife would always be trustworthy.

The second Blaire realized where her thoughts had

led, her eyes narrowed and she gunned the accelerator. When she came to the first stoplight, she reached for her work schedule to see what address was next on the docket.

With the doctor's counseling and strategies, she was getting better at cutting off negative thought processes that dragged her into the hellish black void of a thousand what-ifs. She had to admit it helped when a colleague came out on the job with her.

Since working for the Texas Oak Wilt Suppression Project, she often went out on assignments with one of the other five area resource foresters from the office. This week she and Perry Watkins had teamed up.

She enjoyed the married man's upbeat spirit. A colleague's presence served as a great preventative against introspection. But he'd just left her a text message telling her not to expect him to join her. Earlier this week he'd complained of a toothache. His dentist could fit him in for a root canal. He didn't know how long he'd be.

You're on your own today, Blaire.

She turned on the radio, but the Rachmaninoff concerto playing on the classical FM station touched her core too deeply to keep listening. Blaire had grown up playing the piano. On their first date, Nate had taken her to the symphony where they'd heard "Rhapsody on a Theme of Paganini," one of her favorite pieces.

Her parents had given them a baby grand for their wedding present. After they were married, she went on playing and teaching the children from her old neighborhood while she finished up her college studies. With the extra money she'd bought season tickets for the symphony. If Nate couldn't go, she took a friend or family member. But since the day joy went out of her life, she hadn't touched the piano or attended another concert.

Pressing the scanner, she came to a country-and-Western station, but the poignant lyrics talked about loss. Blaire could have written them.

Other stations were playing nonstop Christmas music. Certain times of the year were more oppressive than others. The thought of Christmas depressed her. She skipped those stations. The scanner stopped on a talk show.

Politics.

Someone else's rage was just the thing to prevent her from dwelling on her eternal state of limbo. She turned up the volume.

CAIGE APPROACHED THE redheaded police officer. "One breakfast coming up. A steak burrito and a lemonade."

Gracie lifted her head. "You're a sweetie!" She got to her feet. "Good luck wading through these." She pointed to five files sitting on her desk. "You can stay in my office. I'm going to the lunchroom to make everyone envious."

He chuckled. "Thanks. I don't know what I'd do without you."

She took the sack and drink from him. "I'd like to think that's true. It would vindicate my existence," she bantered. On a more serious note she asked, "How's Josh?"

"He's terrific."

"And his daddy?"

Caige gave her a frank stare. His black hair was showing glints of gray at the temples. The same gray of his eyes was discernible in the bits of dark stubble on his jaws when he got up to shave every morning. He was close to thirty-four years old, going on a hundred, and she knew it. "He's doing okay."

"I'll take okay, for now." She winked. "We'll be putting up a Christmas tree this week. When all the decorations are done, Sam and I want you to bring Josh over to the house. The girls will love to play with him. I'll call you in a few days."

He felt his throat swell. "That sounds wonderful."

"If I'm not back when you've finished going through these, just leave them on the desk."

"Will do."

"See you later."

After she shut the door, he sat down at her desk. She kept pictures of her husband and two daughters in plain sight. Tricia was ten, Mandy twelve. Both were friendly like their mom. Josh could use all the warmth they were willing to give.

His son didn't have close friends. He'd been only five when the accident had happened. Gracie had been right there with her daughters for support. He honestly didn't know what he would have done without a friend like her.

Mac and the other men in the office had done everything possible to help him out and still did. But a child needed friends his own age. Mrs. Wright assured him the children in his class at school provided a certain amount of necessary interaction. Still…nothing replaced a mother's love.

No matter how much love Caige gave his son, Josh would always need more. When he thought about the future and how uncertain it was, his stomach clenched.

Caige had set his financial affairs in order so that Josh would always be taken care of. But who would love his boy if something happened to him in the line of duty? He'd been thinking that maybe he should quit the Rangers and move to Naylor, a small town northeast of Austin. An hour's drive.

His parents and married siblings lived there. Josh had three cousins he'd played with over the Thanksgiving weekend. Everyone loved him. Caige's parents had been encouraging him to bring their grandson home where they could be on hand all the time. His sister, Rosie, had assured him the Naylor elementary school had an excellent special-education program.

Maybe it was a solution Caige hadn't wanted to accept because it meant a total life change. But he'd do anything for Josh, whose needs would only increase as he got older. During Christmas vacation Caige would have the freedom to set things in motion for the two of them if he decided to move.

It wouldn't alter the situation for Liz, who would always have access to Josh if she wanted. He'd never stop praying for that to happen. As for Caige, he could put the house on the market and buy another one in Naylor. Instead of doing Ranger business, he'd go back to ranching alongside his brother, Kip. The two would also help their father with his ranching as they'd done in their teens.

He stared at the five files, wondering if the Farley case was going to be the last one he ever worked on as a Ranger.

The first case in the stack dealt with a female victim who'd been working at a dry cleaners and had been shot at close range. The other four cases involved male victims; a prisoner being transferred, a security guard at a warehouse, a Realtor found shot in his own office and a golfer found shot on a golf course.

Caige vaguely remembered hearing talk about the death of an Austin golfer who'd turned pro, but Caige had been out of town on another case and hadn't learned the details.

He went through each file making copies of the ballistics reports. When a gun was fired, it left a unique microscopic marking on the bullet and shell casing, much like a human fingerprint. He would ask Dirk in forensics to fire Mr. Farley's gun with Farley's own ammo and compare the bullet and shell casing to the ones in these reports. Maybe there'd be a match. With no leads, it was worth investigating.

After putting back the ballistics report in the last file, he happened to glance at some photographs. There was a graphic picture of the twenty-eight-year-old pro golfer Daniel Reardon Dunn shot in the heart. On the sixth of September he'd been found dead at the eighteenth hole of the Hilly Heights golf course in Austin.

There was another photograph taken at the graveside service for him. Sometimes a detective on a homicide case would decide to take a few pictures at the funeral knowing that a certain percentage of killers showed up to see the victim buried. Among the crowd of thirty or so people standing in the background with the other mourners he spotted Nathan and Blaire Farley.

He made a low whistle. "Well, what do you know."

The photograph hadn't produced results for the other detective, but Caige was encouraged by this find. If Farley was a killer—*this* golfer's killer—not only would it solve the Dunn murder, it would change the whole complexion of the Farley case itself.

He copied the photo, then headed back to the office, catching up with Mac in the hallway. "Can we talk?"

"Sure. Come on in my office."

He followed his boss inside and shut the door. Without preamble he told him what he'd found in the files and handed him the papers. Mac whistled when he saw the photocopy of the Farleys at the graveside service. "Sometimes you come up with something so fast, you give me gooseflesh."

"It may be nothing."

His boss made a strange sound in his throat. "Don't you ever quit on me."

Caige averted his eyes. "Let's get that gun and ammo over to forensics, stat."

"I'll take care of it. Now, tell me about your plan because I know you have one." After working together for so long, there were no secrets between them.

"I'm thinking two weeks undercover as a forester should be enough time for me to get inside Mrs. Farley's mind. If she's innocent, then she doesn't know what she knows and it will be up to me to pick her brains. But if she did have something to do with her husband's disappearance, then I'm counting on her being less paranoid after five years. She's bound to make a slip that's significant."

Mac nodded. "I'll talk to her supervisor and make arrangements for you to chat with him later today if possible. I'll tell him we'd like you on board there by Monday morning."

"Good. However, that means I've only got this weekend to absorb the fundamentals that took her a college education to learn."

"For you it'll be a piece of cake. The rest you can pick up as you go, but I realize you'll be spending most of your time with Josh until Monday. If you want, Mona and I will come over on Sunday and give you a break."

Nobody came any better than Caige's boss, who had grandchildren of his own. "I appreciate the offer, but I'll work it out. Josh loves the park. I can do some studying while we're there. Thanks, Mac."

"HEY, BLAIRE!"

Blaire came all the way into the office and spotted the secretary. "Hi, Sheila! How was your weekend with Tim?" They'd gone to San Antonio.

"Fabulous. I bought a new painting with a Southwest flavor to match my decor."

"That's terrific!"

Blaire's gaze swerved to one of her other colleagues. "Out with it, Marty. How many football games did you watch this weekend?"

"Pam let me see three."

"For that sacrifice, what did you have to do for her?"

"The kids and I went Christmas shopping with her. We hit every store in the Barton Creek Mall."

Blaire chuckled. "I'm sure that made her day."

In truth, Blaire needed to get started on some shopping of her own. Besides her parents, she had her grandparents who lived in Houston; a younger married sister, Gwen; a brother-in-law, Jim; their new baby, Christopher, and the people in her office to buy for. As for her brother, Mark, who'd joined the navy and wasn't married yet, she needed to get gifts off to him right away or he might not receive them by Christmas.

Marty grinned. "So what did *you* do?"

"I've been refinishing a pair of end tables and a coffee table for my living room."

"And?"

"There's no *and.*" Marty never tired of trying to line her up with a great guy he knew. But to date a man who was interested meant having to tell him her situation. Nothing would kill that interest faster, which was all right with her. Blaire wasn't interested, either.

In two more years, if no evidence came forth to the contrary, her father reminded her, she could have Nate declared legally dead. Then at least she could be considered a widow and would be able to marry again if she wanted to, which she didn't.

But there would always be a few people who wondered what had happened to Nate, and still weren't sure how much she really knew about his disappearance. In her case, she didn't need to wear a scarlet letter to be treated with a certain amount of caution and speculation.

She sat down at her desk to check her emails. By the time she'd finished setting up her appointments for the day, the other staff had come through the door. Blaire looked up. "Did you see Perry on your way in?"

They shook their heads.

"He's not coming," Sheila announced. "I just got off the phone with the boss. He said Perry's personal leave came through. He'll be gone for the next two weeks."

"Wow, and right before Christmas. That's amazing."

"Yup. Too bad we can't all be that fortunate."

"I hear you."

Since the guys in the office already had their rotations for the week figured out, it appeared Blaire was going to be on her own. Their boss, Stan Belnap, preferred they work in pairs, but sometimes it wasn't possible.

"In that case, I need to get going, and I'll leave a copy of my appointment sheet with you." She put it on Sheila's desk and headed toward the door. "See you all tomorrow. Everybody have a great day."

"You, too," they called out.

She walked out of the forest service's four-story building and headed for her truck in the parking lot. Her first destination was a convenience store where she could buy some ice for the small ice chest she kept with her. When she took tree samples, she stored them in it to keep cold until she could send them to the lab.

Another half hour of battling morning traffic and she reached her first appointment in southwest Austin. She was supposed to meet Carl, the manager of the Sunset apartment complex, outside his office at eight-thirty.

Once she found the designated parking area, she got out of the cab and walked through the breezeway where she discovered a middle-aged man waiting. "Are you Carl?"

"Yes. You must be Ms. Koslov. Come with me and I'll show you what I'm concerned about."

Four separate buildings faced onto a grove of sycamore trees probably seventy feet high. They walked over to a tree with some brown spots on the fallen leaves. She nodded. "These trees have been attacked by a common disease called anthracnose. The owner of the complex needs to arrange for the trees to be pruned."

The manager shook his head. "He's not going to like it."

"He'll like it a lot less if they die." She pointed to the tops. "Some of those branches need to be removed to allow more sunlight in so the leaves will thrive."

"If you say so. I'll get right on it."

"That's good. These are lovely trees, the focal point of the complex. It would be a shame to lose any of them."

"I agree. Thanks for being so prompt."

"You're welcome." With that accomplished, she drove off to her next appointment ten miles to the east. This time it was the residence of the Johnsons, a couple probably in their early eighties. According to the message, they'd lived in their home on its five-acre lot of live oaks for years.

"Thank you for coming, Ms. Koslov. These are like

our children." Mrs. Johnson stood in the doorway, wringing her hands. Her husband was leaning on a cane while he stared at Blaire with tears in his eyes. She understood their grief. Trees like theirs had to be at least two hundred years old. They were their pride and joy, a living part of them. "Please tell us what we can do to save them."

"First, I have to make an inspection. It might take a while. You stay in the house. When I'm through I'll come back and we'll talk."

Mrs. Johnson bit her lip and whispered her thanks.

Blaire started around the side of the house with her satchel and ice chest. She approached one of the sick-looking trees, noticing a "stag-head" appearance at the crown. The isolated dead branches on top told their own story. She estimated this tree had been infected two or more years.

Oak wilt was a fungus that invaded the tree's vascular system, clogging it and cutting off the water supply. It killed trees. The fungus had been infesting trees across the United States and was responsible for an epidemic in Texas. Ten thousand trees had been lost to date.

Though she saw signs of the disease in the scorched leaves, she needed to take samples and have them analyzed back at the laboratory first to verify her diagnosis. Sometimes symptoms were confused with other causes due to changes in soil grade, root rot, two-lined chestnut borer…the list went on and on.

After getting out a can of disinfectant, she sprayed her hands and the entire contents of her satchel and ice chest inside and out. Once she'd tucked a small can of black spray paint into her back pocket, she took her handsaw and a plastic bag and started climbing the tree.

At a certain point she collected wilted branches that still had some partially green leaves. She gathered half a dozen pieces that were six inches long and a half inch in diameter, leaving the bark on them. A couple of twigs had wilted leaves. She took a few samples of those, too.

Since the fungus was heat-sensitive, the samples needed to be kept cool and analyzed quickly before they dried out. She put everything in the plastic bag, then sprayed the spots where she had cut to prevent further infection.

With that done, she climbed back down to the first joint in the tree. From there she jumped to the ground, almost landing on someone standing at the base. She let out a shocked cry. The saw and plastic bag dropped from her hand.

"Oh—" she said again when two strong, masculine hands reached down to help her up. "I could have injured you."

"But you didn't," a deep male voice said. "Sorry I startled you, Blaire Koslov."

Chapter Two

When Blaire lifted her head, she found herself looking up at a man with medium-cropped black hair and hard-boned facial features. As gradations of rugged male beauty went, his had to be off the charts. Above a chiseled jaw and cheekbones she discovered crystalline gray eyes staring down at her.

They were framed by long lashes as dark as his winged brows—and they reflected male interest. But Blaire felt them probe hers as if he were searching for something. What it was, she didn't know. It sent the strangest sensation through her.

In fact, the way he'd expressed himself just now—his body language, everything about him—gave off an unconscious aura of authority that caught her off guard. For no reason she could think of, she sensed he could be dangerous, too. The situation had made her slightly breathless.

"It's all right. I should have looked before I leaped."

An unexpected little half smile at the corner of his wide mouth threw her further off balance. Blaire was used to being around the guys in their forest service uniforms. But this man had to be six foot two or three, with a hard-muscled physique that made him quite unforgettable. She knew she'd never seen him before.

He sprayed his hands with her disinfectant. Blaire noticed he didn't wear a ring of any kind. Two years after having no word of Nate, she'd taken off her own wedding band and engagement ring. They were in the dresser for safekeeping.

"I thought you must have seen me walking toward you. I'm Jack Lignell with the Trees for Texas program here in Austin." That explained why their paths hadn't crossed. "Your boss sent me to be Perry Watkins's replacement while he's on personal leave. I'm afraid you're stuck with me for the next couple of weeks." He spoke in a low cultured voice she found as attractive as the rest of him.

"That works both ways." She flashed him a smile, trying to seem as normal as possible when she didn't feel normal at all. "Welcome to the team."

"Thank you." As he hunkered down to put the plastic bag in the ice chest, the play of muscles in his shoulders and back drew her gaze. She detected the appealing scent of the soap he must have used in the shower as it mingled with the disinfectant. It wafted past her, increasing her awareness of him.

"How did you know where to find me?"

He stood up. "Sheila, is it? She gave me your schedule. I've been two steps behind you, then I saw the truck in the driveway. Mrs. Johnson told me where to come. Did you know she and her husband were married out here sixty years ago?"

"I had no idea."

So he'd had quite a chat with them. She sensed this take-charge man would certainly have inspired confidence in the owners of this property.

She reached in the satchel for her hammer and chisel to take a sample from the joint of the tree. It required scraping off the bark to get to the woody white tissue. After setting herself to the task, she took a sample and placed it in another plastic bag before spraying the spot with black paint.

He put the bag in the chest with the other one. "Mr. Johnson said they planned on their love going on forever just like these trees. It's nice to meet a couple who've been so devoted to each other over the years."

"I agree." Once upon a time Blaire had planned on a marriage that lasted a lifetime, but instead she'd had a nightmare she'd never awoken from. The last thing she felt like doing was talking about it. "After hearing their story, it's vital we get to the source of the problem in a hurry so as many trees as possible can be preserved."

His eyes studied the other diseased trees before he nodded. "If it turns out this is live oak wilt, the rock saw will have to be brought in to break up those roots and stop the spread."

"The Johnsons won't like it. Did you explain that to them?"

Her question caused his gaze to swerve to hers. "I thought it better not to say anything until we get the lab results back first with a firm diagnosis. I told them it could be two to four weeks." He picked up the ice chest. "I'll tell them goodbye and meet you at your truck."

Blaire studied Perry's replacement as he headed for

the house on those long, powerful legs. One thing she'd already learned about her new temporary partner. The man didn't like to waste time. Neither did she.

After putting all the tools and cans in the satchel, she started walking around the house and discovered him waiting for her with the driver's door open. He'd put the chest on the seat and reached for the satchel to stow it for her.

She wasn't used to help from the guys, but she didn't mind. In fact, it was rather nice. "Thank you."

He nodded. "Since time is of the essence where those samples are concerned, let's drive to College Station and drop them off at the lab."

"I usually courier them on ice overnight."

"I'm aware of that, but I was just pulled off my job at Trees for Texas to fill in. I'd like to pick your brains to get the lay of the land so to speak. Your supervisor, Stan Belnap, said he didn't have the time to do it. I figure our three-hour round trip will give you time to bring me up-to-date on your latest project. Do you mind?"

She blinked. "No. Of course not." What else could she say? It was all in the line of work. It was just that he was the first man to disturb her senses since Nate, and she was so surprised by her feelings, she felt…she felt *stupid*.

Kind of like the way she'd felt in high school when she'd developed her first real crush on a gorgeous guy and didn't know how to handle it. Surely being this close to her thirtieth birthday ought to have matured her emotions.

"Then I'll follow you back to the office and we'll

go from there in the truck they issued me. We'll grab lunch en route. I presume any appointments we miss this afternoon, Sheila can reschedule for tomorrow."

He possessed a rare, unconscious self-assurance she found intriguing despite her effort not to give him any more thought than she gave Perry or her other male colleagues. But the more Blaire tried to concentrate on anything else, the more she found herself unable to.

She climbed into the cab. "I'll give her a call on the way."

"Good," he said with a quick smile and shut her door before walking around to get in his truck.

For the first time in years she was conscious of the pulse throbbing at her throat. She'd already acknowledged the reason for it, but still couldn't believe it. Somehow Blaire had thought that part of her had died when Nate had gone missing.

On her drive back to the office in the northeastern part of Austin, the noon traffic proved to be worse than the morning commute. Yet through all of it, Jack Lignell stayed right behind her. While she spoke to Sheila, she tried not to glance at the rearview mirror, but even with him out of sight, she sensed such an energy in the cosmos from him that she could feel it no matter how much she wished she could ignore him.

After she parked the truck with the rest of the fleet, he was right there to put her things in the back of his truck and help her get in. Their arms brushed by accident, putting an electric seal on the morning's events.

Blaire's doctor had predicted that one day she would come alive again when she least expected it.

As he started up his truck, she wondered if her energy gave off vibes to him. She prayed not.

BLAIRE KOSLOV WAS APPEALING, all right, just as Agent Robbins had intimated. Caige would never forget the stunned look coming from those incredible blue eyes when she'd realized she'd almost jumped on him.

She was nice. Polite. Educated. Businesslike, but not to the extreme.

He'd spotted her curved figure and long legs up in the tree before he'd reached it. She had a lissome quality when she moved. Face-to-face, he found her wide mouth provocative. Her classic features were framed by neck-length wavy hair with a lustrous sheen.

The black-and-white photo hadn't done her justice. In the sunlight her hair reminded him of swirls of caramel sauce poured over vanilla ice cream, not quite mixed together. All in all, Nathan Farley's lovely wife possessed a strong, natural femininity he couldn't remember coming across before in other women.

Caige's first thought was that her missing spouse wouldn't willingly have left her. But that was Caige the *man* speaking, because Blaire Koslov's particular brand of charisma had already gotten under his skin. Not even with Liz had he felt this intense physical attraction to another woman on a first meeting.

But Caige the *Ranger* knew a beautiful spouse had no pull on a husband leading a life dominated by crime. Caige could point to hundreds of cases of beautiful wives being abandoned as proof.

Last but not least, a beautiful spouse could commit

premeditated murder just as easily as any murderer. Caige knew that, too.

Agent Robbins had said he wanted to believe Nathan Farley had been a victim of foul play and that Blaire Koslov was innocent of any wrongdoing. After meeting her, Caige wanted to believe it, too, but his years of training with the Rangers forced him to consider every ugly possibility.

If she'd killed her husband, then he needed to discover a motive. That's where he would concentrate while they drove to College Station, but first they needed food. Twenty miles out of Austin, he pulled into a diner he favored.

After shutting off the motor he turned to her. "Have you ever eaten at Wally's?"

"No, but I've passed it dozens of times on my way home to visit family."

"Way home from where?"

"College Station."

"You lived there?"

"I went to Texas A&M for graduate school."

That piece of information hadn't been in the report because the detectives had dropped the ball in her husband's case before she'd finished her undergraduate studies.

"Did you get a degree?"

"Yes. Plant pathology."

Despite what had happened to her, she'd pursued more education. Innocent or guilty, it proved she had a strong will. "That explains your expertise."

"I don't know about that."

"*I* do. The way you went about performing surgery on that tree joint like a bone surgeon convinced me." Her gentle laugh charmed him. Their eyes held for a moment. "Your supervisor said I could learn a lot from you. He was right."

Blaire's boss had gone out of his way to help Caige cram a lot of knowledge into one weekend of learning time. He gave him a book on tree diseases and marked passages for him to read for the next few nights so he wouldn't be at a complete loss. What he didn't know he could blame on being pulled from the Trees for Texas program, which concentrated on continually planting new trees rather than dealing with tree diseases.

On that note Caige got out of the cab and would have helped her, but she'd already jumped down. After they entered the busy café, he found them a booth and sat across from her. There were menus in the wall holder. He handed her one. "Take a look and let me know what you want. I'll phone it in with mine."

Blaire noticed there were phones on the walls at each booth to call in the order. Once she'd made a decision and he'd placed them, she excused herself. "My hands are covered in disinfectant. I need to wash it off."

"We both do."

In a few minutes they were back. She took the initiative. "Tell me about yourself. Where did you go to college?"

"The University of Texas in Austin."

"So did I. My family's always lived here."

He smiled at her. "After graduation, I started work with the forest service."

"Were you born in Austin, too?"

Though being undercover meant some lies were necessary, he found it better to stick to the truth whenever possible, so he answered, "No. Naylor."

"Oh. I've been there many times with family to check out the museums. That's not far away."

"It's close enough for my son and I to visit family when I get the time off."

He heard her hesitation before she said, "What about your wife?"

It appeared that if he wanted information from Blaire, then he needed to invite her into his confidence. "We've been divorced for two years."

"I'm sorry," she murmured. "How old is your boy?"

"Josh turned eight a month ago."

"How lucky you are to have him." The wealth of emotion behind those words sounded real enough.

"You're right about that. Three years ago he was hit by a car in front of the house. For a while we thought we'd lost him."

"How awful," she whispered with compassion.

"I won't lie to you about that. When Josh did pull through, the doctors told us he would be brain-injured. That was a life-changing experience for the three of us.

"Unfortunately, my wife couldn't handle the pain. Since then she has remarried and visits Josh on occasion. Now you know my life story. The reason I've told you all this is because there might be times when I'll have to leave work early or not come at all depending on his good and bad days."

As she stared at him, tears filled her eyes. Before she

could say anything, the waiter brought their burgers. When he had walked away, she cleared her throat. "Do you have a picture?"

Caige hadn't expected that. "Have you got all day?" He reached in his back pocket for his wallet and handed her the small packet of photos.

She studied each one while they ate. "He's darling. Precious. One day he's going to grow up looking a lot like his dad," she said with a tremor in her voice.

When she handed them back, a lone tear trickled down her cheek. She wiped it with her napkin. "Who takes care of him while you're working?"

"He goes to a special-ed class at school and I have a housekeeper."

Blaire shook her head. "One of my piano students had a sister with neurological damage. She couldn't bear to be out of her mother's sight."

"That's Josh. Every day is like *Groundhog Day,* if you saw the movie."

"You mean each day starts out like the first time, every time. That's what Nancy told me. She's the little girl's mother."

"Except that Josh *is* making progress and walks into the school with me now." Last month's bus incident was a hiccup. "I don't have to pick him up and carry him in."

"But I bet it's agony for you to have to walk away from him."

He nodded, surprised by her insight. "How do you know so much?"

"Because I've watched what happens to Nancy when

she has to leave her daughter." More tears glazed her eyes. "A parent's love is something to behold."

There was a lot of depth to this woman. "When did you start giving piano lessons?"

"I took piano from an early age and loved it. Music was my world. By high school I was giving lessons to the kids in the neighborhood."

"You must have been outstanding."

"Don't I wish."

"I'm impressed." He drank the rest of his coffee, anxious to get to know her better. He kept telling himself it was because he had a case to solve, nothing more. But already he found himself interested in Blaire for personal reasons. This shouldn't be happening on the job. It never had before....

"What about you, Blaire? Do you have children? I don't see a ring on your finger."

"I-I'd rather not talk about myself," she stammered, putting down her half-eaten hamburger.

Fear, paranoia—all that and more was wrapped up in her defensive remark. After five years, Caige hadn't expected her to sound this stressed. It was almost as if her husband's disappearance had happened yesterday. He was beginning to understand why the Koslovs had said the disappearance was ruining her life.

"Then we won't. Just because we'll be working together for a couple of weeks doesn't mean you owe me any explanations."

He heard her take a deep breath. "I didn't mean to be rude." If he wasn't mistaken, there was a hint of anguish in those blue depths, arousing his curiosity.

"No offense taken. Would you like dessert before we leave?"

"I can't finish all this, but thank you anyway."

Caige ordered sour apple pie, the best item on the menu. After he'd swallowed the last mouthful, he paid the bill and walked Blaire out of the diner. He couldn't blame the male customers for staring at her. It had been hard not to do it himself.

In another minute they'd taken off once more for their destination. Even without looking at her, he could tell Blaire wasn't at ease. She shifted in the seat several times, recrossing her long, gorgeous legs. He needed to get her talking about something else.

"Tell me about the project we're working on."

"You pretty much know everything already. We're trying to save as many trees as we can. On Thursday we'll be speaking to a large group of Realtors about the Forest Legacy Program. You know, making sure that when land is bought or sold, the trees remain so that the existing forest isn't endangered. You've been working for the Trees for Texas program. With your knowledge you'll be able to add valuable input on the subject of stewardship."

That remained to be seen, he mused. For the rest of the trip Blaire went over what they would discuss using the department's PowerPoint presentation. There'd be plenty of slides with facts and statistics to provide back-up material. He'd call Stan Belnap tonight and get filled in on the legal details of the presentation. By the time they'd reached College Station, they'd exhausted the subject.

In the restroom at the diner, he'd taken the time to look up directions to the lab on his smartphone. When they reached the campus, he was able to drive them to the plant diagnostic lab at the AgriLife extension service as if he did it every day. Recognizing that she wanted some space, he handed her the ice chest and told her he'd wait while she delivered the bags.

With her out of earshot, he leaned against the truck and phoned Mac. "Any news from Dirk yet?"

"No. My guess is he'll have the ballistics report tomorrow. How are things going for Jack Lignell?"

"So far it's working, but this is only the first day."

"Just so you know, when I'm not available I've assigned Ernie to be your contact. He's been brought up-to-date on the case."

"Good." Caige had worked well with the veteran Ranger many times before and since his retirement. "Talk to you later." As he hung up, Blaire came out of the building. When she reached him, he took the chest from her and put it in back while she climbed in her side.

Once they got going again, he glanced at her. "It's warmed up and we're coming to a convenience store. I feel like a drink. Would you like one, too?"

"Nothing for me, thanks."

He pulled to a stop and went inside for a diet cola. In case she changed her mind, he grabbed a bottle of water. While he was on his way to the counter, he reached for a couple of chocolate bars and a pack of Josh's favorite orange gum. When the day was done, Caige liked to take something home to his son.

After he got back in the truck, he opened the sack and put it in front of her. "Take anything you want."

A half smile broke the corner of her mouth. "You don't give up." She opted for the water.

Pleased by this much progress he pulled out the cola and put the sack between them. "One thing you'll learn about me, I don't like drinking alone. For another, when I was married, my wife would always tell me she didn't want something I bought to eat or drink. But two minutes later she was asking for a bite of it, or a sip."

The woman at his side chuckled. "I know exactly what you mean. Thank you for being so thoughtful." Her smile remained as she undid the lid and they both drank. By the time he'd finished his can of soda, she'd emptied half her bottle. He put the empty can in the sack and they headed back to Austin. So far he hadn't got her to open up about her husband.

"When we get home, will you have a load of piano students waiting for you?"

It took her a long time to answer. "Not anymore." He noticed her hand tighten around the neck of the bottle. "I stopped giving lessons five years ago."

"Because of school?"

"No."

"After what you told me about your love of music, I have to admit I'm surprised."

When she didn't offer anything else, Caige realized he was almost out of tricks. "Then tell me some more about the Texas Oak Wilt Suppression Project."

At first he thought he'd made her angry. Then suddenly she broke down and laughed. The sound pleased him no end. "I bet you drove your mother crazy."

He grinned, liking the fact that she didn't take herself too seriously. "You don't want to know."

She sat straighter in the seat. "Since we have to work together, it's only natural we know a few basic things about each other. But once I tell you about me, you might not want to work with me and I wouldn't blame you."

"Then how come Stan Belnap told me I was going to like this job?"

"He's paid to say things like that."

Caige reached in the sack for a candy bar and started eating it. "If you're willing to tell me, I'd really like to hear. We've still got some miles to go. I'll be honest and admit that I don't feel like talking every minute about *Ceratocystis fagacearum, Phytophthora* foot rot, *Hypoxylon* canker or any other tree disease you can think of."

He'd hoped to get another smile out of her, but she stared glumly out the passenger window. "You might prefer it to knowing I'm a person of interest to the police and have been for the last five years."

"That's quite a statement."

"There's more. My last name's Farley, but I go by my maiden name, Koslov, for less notoriety. My father's Russian great-grandparents settled here. Some of their things are in the Russian Heritage Museum in Naylor."

He'd gone to see it many times as a boy. *That's* what she'd meant about museums. The part of her blood that was Russian might account for her rare kind of beauty.

"What happened five years ago?"

"The husband I loved disappeared one day as if into thin air."

The husband she loved.

That clear, simple, pure declaration, told to a man she had no idea was a Texas Ranger, rang in Caige's ears.

"Until his body is found alive or dead," she went on speaking, "I'm someone they continually watch in case I killed him or helped kill him or have knowledge of his whereabouts."

Caige felt as though he was hearing all this for the first time. "And I thought *I* went through hell three years ago."

She turned her head in his direction. Her face was a study in pain. "If there were a better word than *hell,* I'd use it. The night he didn't make it home, I'd fixed a special dinner for him to mark our wedding anniversary. We'd been married eight months. I'm not saying it was a perfect marriage, or that there weren't moments of doubts and fears, but I have to admit I didn't see it coming."

"No one could see something like that coming," Caige said. He hadn't seen Josh's accident or the aftermath coming. After it happened, three lives had been turned upside down.

"When the police interrogated me, I couldn't believe they thought I might have had anything to do with his disappearance. I was incredibly naive back then. Over the last five years I've learned enough and read enough to understand it's part of their job to be suspicious, but it's been a bitter pill to swallow."

He heard the suffering in her voice, except it went much deeper than that. He heard unspeakable sorrow, disbelief, bewilderment, defeat, anger and loss beyond tears. For a minute he felt as if he'd gotten inside her skin.

"The police couldn't have a case against you or you wouldn't be working for the forest service."

"That's true, but an invisible finger has always been pointed at me, and not just by the authorities. It's okay. I've lived with it for a long time."

It had to be agony for her every time she had to tell her story to a new guy wanting a relationship with her. He understood why she'd closed up on him at first.

"Naturally the subject comes up whenever a man wants to get to know you better," Caige muttered more to himself than to her. He could imagine there'd been many men over the past five years wanting a relationship with her. "Does everyone in the office know?" The guys in the office wouldn't be immune.

"I'm sure Stan's told them, but it hasn't put Marty off. He keeps trying to line me up, but I always tell him no. My life's a joke right now. What man wants to know I *could* be Nate Farley's widow, but maybe I'm not? Maybe he was kidnapped and he's still trying to get back to me—or maybe he isn't.

"Maybe he struck his head and has amnesia and is wandering around close by. Maybe he wanted his freedom without going through a divorce, so he checked out of life and commited suicide in the middle of the ocean. Maybe he died of natural causes in a place that has yet to be discovered. Or maybe he was murdered in cold blood and his body is in a landfill."

Her head reared back. "The maybes are endless and five years gives you an eternity to think of the possibilities."

She was right about that. "Did you know him for a long time before you were married?"

"No. We met and married within six months."

"Were you planning on a family?"

"One day. When he first disappeared, part of me wished I'd insisted on getting pregnant right away even if I was still in school. Nate thought it would be better if we waited until I graduated. From a financial point of view it made sense. But after he was gone, I thought how much easier the loss would have been to handle if I'd had a baby."

She drank the rest of her water. "After a year had passed, I was grateful I didn't have a child to raise. Without having to worry about anyone but myself, I was able to go to graduate school. I consoled myself that in an ideal world a little boy or girl needed both parents, something I couldn't provide."

"Yup," he muttered. She'd hit on the very problem Caige had been wrestling with since Liz had left.

"Oh, I'm sorry if I said anything to hurt you—" she blurted, sounding so penitent it humbled him. Her soul-filled eyes got to him.

"You didn't. Like you, I've had to learn to live with certain facts of life."

At this point Caige didn't like trying to find out if she'd had a part in getting rid of her other half. In fact, he didn't like living a lie, no matter if everything else he'd told her was the truth. Until now he'd never felt any guilt for going undercover in the line of duty. This was a new one on him.

"Your boss didn't say anything to me about your personal life. He only told me you were the best forester he'd ever had working for him."

"He's a sweet liar and probably held back details about my private life because you're a temp." She put the empty bottle in the sack. "Sorry I've been difficult. Tomorrow we'll start fresh."

The one thing Blaire hadn't done was assert her innocence. He had a hunch that no matter how long he waited, he wouldn't hear it from those tempting lips. If he were in her shoes, he'd be the same way. Righteous indignation would stop you from insisting that you hadn't done anything wrong.

They'd arrived back at the office. He parked the truck and carried the ice chest to her car in the other parking lot. She got in with her satchel and put down her window. Some of the shadows had gone from those blue eyes. "Thank you for lunch."

Don't let things get personal, Dawson. "You can buy it for us tomorrow."

"Sounds good. See you at eight. But if there's a problem because of Josh, don't worry about it. You can catch up to me if you have to. Sheila always has a copy of my work schedule."

"I'll keep that in mind."

For the first time in so long he couldn't remember, he was looking forward to eight o'clock tomorrow morning. Before getting in his car, he watched her drive away.

Since morning Caige had been looking for a motive to prove she might have had something to do with her husband's disappearance, but so far he hadn't stumbled across anything to make him doubt her love for her husband. It seemed the opposite held true.

But her comment that Farley hadn't wanted to start a family right away could mean something, or nothing at all. The average person wouldn't think about it one way or the other. Caige had to consider everything. Since Farley had disappeared, Caige was forced to consider what other motive besides lack of money might have prompted him to want to put off fatherhood.

More time alone with his wife? Not wanting the responsibility of being a parent yet? Did being an only child make the thought of having a baby with Blaire less of a priority? Had he been a selfish man? Narcissistic, even?

Agent Robbins had made a comment about something Mrs. Koslov had said that had stuck with Caige. Her son-in-law was a self-starter. It was a great quality that could lead to greater things, or it could get a person in trouble depending on certain character traits.

How hungry was Farley for the things he hadn't been given in life?

Unless there'd been a fund set up by his family years earlier, a grandmother on a fixed income didn't give a smart, good-looking young man the kinds of perks he might have received from a well-heeled father, for example. Caige didn't know nearly enough about Farley, but he was determined to find out.

He reached for his cell and called Mac. "I'll need a warrant to go through the Farleys' bank-account records. I want to see if any of the half-dozen names of friends and coworkers his wife had mentioned in the police report might have done business at the same bank. In case any of them did, I'm curious to see what might turn up. You never know."

"You're right about that."

"Do me a favor and ask the judge to fill it out for tomorrow morning when the Yellow Rose campus branch opens at nine. I'll need a couple of hours."

"You've got it. Anything else?"

"Not for now. Thanks, Mac." He hung up.

After spending the day with Blaire, he would stake his reputation as a Ranger that she was innocent of any wrongdoing. Unfortunately, he was going on gut feeling, not hard evidence. For him to get emotionally involved with her went counter to everything his profession warned against, but by the time he pulled into his driveway, he recognized he already was involved in a way he shouldn't be. This was a complication he didn't need right now.

Damn.

He hurried into the house to give his son a big hug and spend time with him. Josh loved games. Caige hid the gum he'd brought under a book on the coffee table. He played warm and hot with him. By the time Elly had dinner ready, his boy had uncovered his prize.

Chapter Three

Blaire left the Arboretum Shopping Center two hours later feeling relief that she'd gotten Mark's gift sent off. Because he was in the navy, it had been hard to pick the right present for him. In the end she'd decided to send him a care package with all kinds of little things he could use and enjoy.

It hadn't been easy for her when he'd first left home two years ago. After Nate's disappearance, her brother had been there for her every step of the way. Though he was still supportive, it wasn't the same knowing he was so far away.

The shopping expedition had provided a good distraction to get her mind off Jack Lignell. It had been at least a year since she'd been forced to talk about Nate to anyone, but it had been easy with him.

Her parents were the ones who kept in touch with the last detective assigned to Nate's case. Normally when she had to relive the horror of it, she felt drained afterward, but not tonight. Right now she felt exhilarated.

After letting herself inside her small two-story town house, she was ready for a long soak in the tub. A half hour later she got into bed with her laptop and added notes on today's business to her files. It was necessary to jot down the exact time she'd extracted the samples and the time they'd been dropped off, in case there was any question about them.

As she closed the file, her cell phone rang. She glanced at the caller ID and clicked on.

"Hi, Mom."

"Hi, darling. I thought I'd hear from you before now."

Either Blaire's mother or father checked in with her every night, or she phoned them. It was a ritual that made her feel safe and helped her parents cope. But tonight she'd forgotten. "After work I went to the Arboretum to get off Mark's gift. Now I'm just finishing up business. Sorry if I worried you."

"You didn't. I was out doing some Christmas shopping myself. I bought your brother a new iPhone."

"He'll *love* it. Marty has one. You can do anything with them."

"So I found out. The sales rep spent at least an hour showing me everything. By the time he was through, I decided to buy us each one."

"You're kidding! Thank you! I know Gwen and Jim have been wanting one. They'll be thrilled."

"I agree. Meet me for lunch tomorrow and I'll give you yours early."

Jack had mentioned lunch tomorrow.

"I'd love that, but could we make it on Wednesday instead? How about the Iron Cactus at twelve-thirty? I'll arrange my schedule so we can have a full hour to play around with them."

"Wonderful. Your father insists he likes his old ten-dollar phone just fine, so don't let on about his until Christmas."

"Absolutely. I'll call you tomorrow. Love you, Mom."

She hung up, glad her mother hadn't asked her how her day had gone. Blaire was trying hard not to think about it. But when she turned out the light and burrowed under the covers, she discovered a feeling of excitement she hadn't known in years. It was lighting her up against her will and there was nothing she could do about it.

The feeling was still with her when she arrived at work the next morning and started making out her schedule for the day. Every time one of the guys walked in, she expected it to be Jack. By eight-fifteen she needed to be on her way and left a copy of her route and addresses with Sheila.

The sun didn't shine quite as brightly as she made her way out to the truck. Jack had warned Blaire. This was probably one of Josh's bad days. Somehow when she'd left for the office this morning, she hadn't expected it would suddenly turn out to be one of hers, too.

Yesterday had been a surprise that had knocked her sideways. Blaire wished it hadn't happened. She didn't like feeling alive again because the letdown was excruciatingly painful.

THE MANAGER OF THE CAMPUS branch of the Yellow Rose Bank of Texas met Caige at the door of his private office at nine and shook his hand. "It's an honor to meet one of our Texas Rangers, Mr. Dawson."

"Thank you for helping me with this investigation, Mr. Lawrence."

"It's my pleasure. Come in to this other office. I have everything waiting for you."

Caige followed him.

"Go ahead and sit down at the desk. I hope I've downloaded the right information requested in the judge's warrant. You can read everything from this computer."

"I appreciate you setting things up for me so fast."

"Happy to do it. I'm only sorry that no one in this branch, including myself, ever met or knew Mr. Farley."

"That's not a concern. I have the depositions taken from all the banking people who worked here at the time."

"Of course. Since then, there have been quite a few transfers and turnovers because of the recession."

"Understood."

"If you need anything, just ask."

Once he'd closed the door, Caige got busy. According to the police report of Farley's work record, he'd started mowing lawns at a city golf course from the age of sixteen on and had started banking with Yellow Rose at the same time, but at a different branch.

When he'd attended UT Austin, he'd taken out student loans to get through school. It appeared he'd quit the golf-course job and gotten hired to work part-time in a sporting-goods store and mow lawns at a private country club on weekends. He'd continued to work those jobs after receiving his finance degree.

Three months prior to his marriage to Blaire, Farley had applied for a bank-teller job at the campus branch and was hired at a starting salary of $25,000, with no negative history at any of his past jobs. From that point he did all his banking business at the campus branch. Once he married Blaire, she was added to his checking account, but they maintained separate savings accounts.

Caige was looking for anything that sent up a red flag. He started going through Farley's own banking record first.

In his ten-year history of banking with Yellow Rose, Caige saw no evidence of unexplained large deposits of money, nor unexplained withdrawals of large sums in either the checking or savings accounts. He'd started paying off his student loans after graduation and was diligent about it. If he'd received funds prior to his grandmother's death, they hadn't been deposited in this bank.

During the months Farley had worked at the campus branch, Caige noted the usual credit-card usage for various restaurants, purchases from local shops and stores. There were a dozen debits for charges from a travel agency. Maybe he'd traveled for the bank. Caige printed out everything so he could go over each item later.

Then he turned to the police report on Blaire. She'd banked at her parents' credit union from the time she was eighteen. The printouts the police had done from that bank showed no irregularities. When she got married, she closed out her account and opened one at Yellow Rose with her husband.

As Caige scrolled through her account, he could see her transactions were consistent with the finances for her schooling and earned income from giving piano lessons. After her husband's disappearance, the police report indicated she closed out her checking and savings accounts at Yellow Rose, and went back to the credit union. Nothing on the printouts from that time forward showed any unusual activity.

So far the two of them looked squeaky clean on paper. The police report contained copies of their income taxes filed every year on time with small tax returns reported. Unlike many newlyweds, they were temperate in their spending and always paid their rent on time.

Having satisfied himself on that score, Caige was curious to know if he'd find anything on the list of names who'd been listed as friends or coworkers of Farley in the police report.

He started with the *A*s, taking notes as he went. It didn't surprise him to see huge blocks of money move in and out of various checking and savings accounts with some of the student accounts. A lot of high rollers banked at the campus branch.

Two of the people who'd worked with Farley at the bank had also banked here, too. Caige quickly scanned their debits and credits, but he didn't see anything unusual.

Caige kept scrolling through the accounts, looking for the next name on the list. While he was searching for a Ben Dykstra, he suddenly muttered, "Bingo—" because Daniel Reardon Dunn's name had just entered his line of vision.

The murdered man's savings account for the last year up to his death had amounted to $6,500,000.

That was an impossible amount of money to be earned by a golfer only recently turned pro!

Seventy percent of the deposits had been made in cash, which meant dirty money was involved. In a one-month period, he'd made two separate cash deposits of $600,000. There was a lot of illegal gambling money floating around Austin.

It was perhaps during the eleven months Farley had worked here that he'd become acquainted with Dunn. Caige wondered if the golfer had hidden money in other banks besides this one. Further scrutiny of the account disclosed he'd withdrawn the entire cash amount and closed out his account on September 4, two days before he'd been found murdered on the golf course.

Caige's mind reeled.

If Farley had been the one to handle that withdrawal, it provided a motive for the Dunn murder, particularly when Farley had disappeared just over two months later, possibly absconding with the cash. But Caige needed the ballistics report from Dirk's office before he could jump to that conclusion.

For Farley, a recent college graduate who only earned $25,000 a year, the temptation to step over the line might have been too great. It was possible Farley had wanted to make a fast buck and had ended up a victim of foul play like Dunn.

Though a long shot, it was worth investigating because one thing was certain. There'd been a connection between Dunn and Farley. The photograph of Blaire and her husband at the graveside established as much.

Maybe Farley's relationship with Dunn had resulted in an under-the-counter deal with mobsters that had gone wrong and he'd been bumped off like Dunn. What

Caige needed was to find out when and where they'd met each other. He would have to get Blaire's input for that because she hadn't put Dunn's name on the list of her husband's friends.

Caige scrolled through the rest of the accounts, looking for the last name on the list compiled by the police, Sheldon Peterson. But he hadn't banked at the Yellow Rose. He shook his head when he happened to come across a checking account where $1,000,000 went in every month. The deposits were made by electronic transfer from a bank in La Jolla, California.

How would it be to have that kind of money sitting in your account...?

One thing was certain: nothing had sent up a warning like the Dunn account. Now that Caige had exhausted his search, he closed the file. Knowing he was onto something big one way or another, he thanked Mr. Lawrence for his help and left the bank.

From the truck, he phoned Sheila for the address of Blaire's next appointment and found himself exceeding the speed limit to join her. Though he was anxious to get answers from her, he recognized something of a personal nature was also driving him.

As he exited the freeway close to his destination, his cell phone rang. He clicked on. "Ernie? What have you got for me?"

"Dirk faxed over the results of the ballistics report you've been waiting for. None of the deaths were the result of bullets fired from Nathan Farley's gun."

Somehow he'd known it would have been too easy if

there'd been a match. "Thanks for the info, Ernie. Talk to you later."

When he turned the next corner, he spotted Blaire's truck on the right. She'd parked in front of a private residence where three large white oaks grew in the front yard. Because she was seated in the cab, he didn't know if she'd just gotten there, or was wrapping up. One of the trees had some large swellings on the limbs and trunk.

Before she made a move, he put down the passenger window and drove up alongside her. She was on the phone, but when she saw him, he could have sworn her eyes lit up before she rang off.

"Hi," he said, trying to tamp down the thrill he felt just looking at her. "How about taking me to lunch when you're through here?"

Her smile got to him. "You caught me in time. I was just leaving." She sounded a little breathless, exactly the way he felt. "What are you in the mood for?"

She'd be surprised. "I'll let you pick the place today."

"You're on. Follow me."

Two miles away she pulled into Ribs Galore where you could eat all the baby back ribs you wanted. Despite the restaurant being crowded, service was fast. As soon as the hostess showed them to a table, a waitress was right there to take their orders and bring them iced tea.

After they were alone, Caige smiled at her. "How did you know?"

"Do you think there's anyone who doesn't love ribs?"

He took a long, refreshing swallow. "I can't comprehend it. So tell me. Were the burls in that white oak caused by fungus?"

"No. When I chiseled through one, I realized it was a case of the wood growing naturally over some young buds."

"That's good. It means they won't lose the tree."

"No. I told the owner he can prune it or call a specialist to remove them by surgery."

He nodded. "Sorry I couldn't join you earlier."

By now they'd been served their ribs and salad. Her eyes searched his. "Did Josh have a hard time this morning?"

"Not any more than usual. The truth is, I had an appointment I couldn't miss. Forgive me."

"No problem."

"I'll still let the boss know. Something else might come up again. Now that my son is getting older, I'm thinking of putting my house up for sale and moving back to Naylor to be near family. It'll probably happen sometime after the first of the year. I'll buy a small ranch there, but it means getting my affairs in order first."

She averted her eyes. "Will you still work for the forest service?"

"No. I grew up ranching and plan to go back to it. I know it will make Josh happier if I'm close at hand all the time. He'll love following me around when he's not at school. Leaving Austin will be good for him."

IF SOMETHING WAS TOO GOOD to be true, then it usually was.

Blaire had only known Jack Lignell two days, but already he'd made such a strong impression on her, the thought that he would be leaving Austin in another month came as an unpleasant shock. Naylor might be only an hour away, but when two people had jobs and responsibilities, the reality of getting together on a daily basis wasn't on.

What had she been thinking?

His unexpected entry into her life had done something terrible to her. Because of him she had realized what a wasteland she'd been living in. When he left, her life would go back to being just that.

She ate the rest of her meal, but, to coin an ancient phrase, the salt had lost its savor.

"What are you doing after work?" The question seemed to come out of the blue and gave her heart a jolt of a different kind.

"I need to do some more Christmas shopping."

"I do, too, but after we passed that miniature golf course on the way here, I thought it might be kind of fun for Josh. I've never taken him to one before. How would you like to meet us there?"

She lifted her eyes to him. "I think it sounds fun." Blaire surprised herself that she could sound so calm about it.

The warmth of his gaze seeped inside her. "In that case let's hurry and get through our afternoon appointments. How many are there?"

"Only three stops on our way back to the office."

"Perfect."

Blaire gave the waitress her credit card to pay the bill before they took off in separate trucks. She didn't remember her wheels touching the ground.

In all three cases, oak wilt appeared to be the culprit. They climbed trees and took samples in record time. While they worked, she asked him questions about Josh. The more she learned, the more she marveled at his coping skills. He had to be a father in a million.

After express-mailing the samples on ice to the lab, they arrived back at the office at four. He walked her to her car. "I'll run home for Josh and meet you at the course in an hour."

She nodded. "That will give me time to change out of my uniform."

"I'd pick you up, but I'd rather not spring anything new on him."

"I understand."

"He's not good in crowds where there are loud noises and flashing lights, but getting there at the dinner hour might mean less people around. We'll see how long he can handle it."

She hoped Josh lasted a long time. On her way home she changed her mind half a dozen times trying to decide what to wear. This would be the first time since Nate that she was meeting a man when it wasn't related to her husband's disappearance or the forest-service business.

After a quick shower she finally decided on her designer jeans and a dusky-blue crewneck cotton sweater with three-quarter sleeves. She ran a brush through her hair and applied fresh-pink-frost lipstick, then slipped into her bone-colored sandals.

Normally she didn't wear any scents on the job in order to keep the insects away, but this was different.

She gave a little poof of her spring flowers eau de toilette and left the town house, eager to see Jack and meet his boy.

When Blaire reached the parking lot at the mini golf course, she realized she was early. While she waited, she phoned her mom to confirm their date for lunch the next day. They chatted for a few minutes about other Christmas presents they needed to get. As she hung up, she spotted Jack's red Toyota turn into the parking area. There were only a few cars around so far. That ought to please Jack.

She got out and walked over to his car while he was undoing Josh's seat belt. To someone who knew nothing about Josh, he would look like any darling eight-year-old wearing a black-and-purple shirt, jeans and sneakers. It wasn't until he climbed down and clung to his daddy's hand to stay close to him that she saw a difference from normal behavior.

The resemblance to his handsome father in his dark hair and striking facial features squeezed her heart. Josh was lean and would probably grow up to be tall like him, too. Jack's gray gaze swept over Blaire, making her legs go weak. "Hi, again. Meet my terrific son, Josh."

While the boy hugged his father's side, she fought not to tear up at hearing the emotion in his voice. "Hello, Josh. I'm happy to meet you. My name's Blaire."

She didn't expect an answer back. While they'd been climbing trees earlier, Jack had told her Josh's speech hadn't returned yet, but the doctor was hopeful. Sometimes he made noises. The three of them walked over to the office located in a miniature Victorian dollhouse. Jack paid the entry fee and they were given some clubs.

He handed her one, but kept his and Josh's until they'd walked to the first hole. With infinite patience he showed Josh what to do with the club and the ball. As it turned out, Josh preferred trying to shove the ball, but he lost interest quickly when he couldn't connect. "Come on, buddy. You'll get it next time."

They made the rounds with Josh holding his father's hand. He stayed so close to him on the runways, Jack could never get off a real shot. Blaire didn't have an excuse and laughed at her own embarrassing score. "I'm terrible at this."

While he stood behind Josh showing him how to swing, Caige flashed her a grin. "Join the club. Have you ever been golfing?"

"If you mean on a real golf course, Nate took me a couple of times. Golf was his passion. In high school he got a job at the municipal golf course mowing lawns so he could play and watch the better players. Eventually he worked at the Hilly Heights Country Club doing lawns and became a caddy. Sometimes he caddied for really good golfers and eventually for a golfer who'd turned pro. In lieu of payment, he gave him private lessons."

"That was a great trade-off. Who was it?"

"Danny Dunn."

Jack frowned. "I think I've heard the name before."

She nodded. "He died ten weeks before my husband's disappearance."

"Now I remember reading something about it in the paper."

Lines broke out on her face. "Yes. It was horrible. Nate had a theory about the reason for the murder, but he never told the police because he had no proof. It would have been pure speculation on his part."

"What was his theory?"

A sigh escaped her lips. "That it might have happened over a lover's quarrel."

"Had your husband met the woman?"

Blaire shook her head. "Nate said that Mr. Dunn was gay, but no one knew it. Once in a while he'd hear him talking to his professional caddy, Ron. Something about their conversation made him think they might have had a liaison."

"Your husband was probably right."

"Nate took his death very hard. It wasn't just a case of looking up to him. Mr. Dunn had told him that if he ever got his golf game to a certain level, he'd help him with the application process to become a pro. I went to the graveside service with Nate. It was tragic to think the golf world had lost someone so promising."

Jack nodded. "Being that Mr. Dunn was his mentor, it would have been especially hard on your husband. He must have picked up a lot of pointers from him, as well as a fabulous golf swing. Did you ever meet the pro?"

"No. Nate didn't want to presume on their relationship. I know he was invited to a party at Mr. Dunn's home in Hyde Park, but it was a one-time invitation."

"I can understand that. Even a minor celebrity can feel hounded by fans."

"Exactly. Though I would have liked to say I met him once, it was never the right time with Nate's and my busy schedules. I had recitals to set up on a regular basis for my piano students. He had to fit in his private lessons with Mr. Dunn early in the morning before he went to work.

"As you can tell, I don't have any skill or patience for this game." She made one more attempt to sink a putt, but missed by a yard. "You see?" She smiled in defeat.

Jack took a turn after her, but was off by a foot. "I think maybe we both need to pick another sport."

She cocked her head. "If your son would let me hold his hand, I bet you could tear this place up."

"You know what?" He leveled an amused glance on her. "I'd rather leave you thinking I'm Tiger Woods." If that was his polite way of saying he didn't think his son would like it, she totally understood. He was Josh's whole world.

"At least Phil Mickelson anyway," she quipped.

Their eyes held. "Did your husband always have ambitions to turn pro one day?"

"Definitely. He loved everything about the golf world and was an encyclopedia of information on the top pro golfers. He chose our apartment because it was close to the Hancock golf course and spent every spare second there when he could."

Somehow it didn't bother her to talk about all this with Jack. "When he was a boy, there was a man living next to his grandmother who took him golfing a few times and it became his raison d'être."

"That was a kind thing for the neighbor to do. What about his father?"

"Nate's parents died in a car accident when he was a baby. His grandparents raised him, but he lost his grandpa when he was ten. But enough of talking about him. What about you and your father?"

Jack smiled. "I'm afraid my dad's love of bull riding didn't catch on with me."

"What were you good at?" She was fascinated by him.

"I did some wrestling, but I'm afraid my great love was motorcycles. I got that from *my* grandfather. After I bought my first one, I banged it up so badly, it ended up in the motorcycle cemetery." She burst into laughter. "Once I'd earned enough money to buy another one, I beat it up, too. In fact, I think it was in the shop more often than not. All I wanted to do was take off and ride."

"You and most of the male population. Do you still have one?"

"I did until Josh's accident. After that I sold it."

He didn't have to explain. His son needed a full-time father who didn't take risks. "Josh would thank you if he could."

Jack's head went back. He stared hard at her. "You think?"

"I know," she whispered. "Your relationship with him touches my heart."

The more she was around him, the less she understood his ex-wife. But since Blaire's marriage hadn't lasted long enough to start a family, she had no way of knowing what it would be like to be a mother and then have to suffer through such a tragedy.

When Nate had disappeared, Blaire hadn't thought anyone's pain could be worse than hers. But that was before she'd met this wonderful boy who needed his father desperately. It was opening her eyes to the pain his mother must have gone through and always would.

Meeting Jack, watching him interact with his son, had opened up a whole new world of understanding to Blaire. He'd lost his wife. His son had lost his mother. Blaire could weep for the situation, but Jack was more than coping with what life had handed him. She wished she were as strong. He made her want to snap out of the malaise she'd let stifle her for so long.

"I bet Josh would like some ice cream. What do you think?"

Jack smiled at her. "He loves chocolate milk shakes."

"Then let's all get one. My treat."

"Did you hear that, bud?" They walked back to the entrance and returned the clubs before heading to their cars. After he used the remote to unlock his, she opened the back door so he could help Josh inside. Once his son was all fastened, Jack shot her a glance. "Follow me. I'll find us a drive-in."

"Okay." She looked inside the car. "See you in a minute, Josh." His son was rocking in the seat.

"He's excited," Jack explained.

"For the ice cream?"

"For that *and* the drive. He loves to go for rides in the car. After work I take him for one every night before he goes to bed."

"That sounds fun to me. See you in a few minutes."

"Drive safely, Blaire," he cautioned.

Though it was something people often said to each other coming and going, with Jack there was more meaning behind it. "That goes for you, too." She was afraid her voice throbbed just then.

Chapter Four

"Mac?"

Caige's boss was just getting off the phone and looked up from his desk. When he saw who it was, he smiled. "Come on in."

He shut the door. "While Blaire's having lunch with her mother, I came over here to get a little work done before I pick her up to go out on our afternoon calls." Caige had let Blaire off in front of the Iron Cactus, telling her to take an hour and a half. They could work late to make up the lost time. He'd already checked with Elly to be sure it was all right with her.

"Sit down and bring me up-to-date."

"The ballistics report didn't link Farley's gun to the Danny Dunn murder or the other four, but there has to be a reason he bought one. I'm hoping Blaire will reveal it during the natural course of conversation."

"How's *that* coming?"

"Last night she told me her husband was a good golfer who used to caddy privately for Dunn. Apparently he learned a lot from his idol in the process and was paid by getting lessons while he caddied for him. That's why he and Blaire went to the funeral. The police working on Dunn's case need to know Farley told his wife he thought Dunn was murdered over a lover's quarrel."

Mac's brows went up.

"You know what they say," Caige murmured. "Caddies hear more stuff than a father confessor. Maybe his lover killed him for the money."

"What money?"

"The $6,500,000 he withdrew from the Yellow Rose Bank of Texas campus branch two days before he was murdered. He had a home in Hyde Park, so that should tell you a lot."

"What?"

"Farley's theory about who killed the golfer should be followed up. He believed Dunn's lover might have been his professional caddy, a guy named Ron."

Mac shook his head before chuckling. "We need to clone you."

Caige made a scoffing sound. "On the outside hunch that Farley's alive and doing target practice somewhere, I talked to the sketch artist downstairs. She's working up a drawing from one of the photographs in his file. He's five years older now and may look different or have dyed his hair. After she puts a flyer together that will include her drawing plus several photo images, Ernie will circulate it to every shooting range in Travis County. Maybe someone has seen him around. It's possible he took someone along with him who could be important to this case. If no ID is made, I'll expand it to include all of Texas.

"In the meantime I've copied his and Blaire's bank

statements for the period he started working at the Yellow Rose until his disappearance. So far the withdrawals and deposits aren't suspicious, but I'll go through them line by line and might come up with something that could give me a lead in a different direction."

Mac studied him for a minute. "What's your instinct about Blaire Farley?"

He sucked in his breath. "I think she's as pure as the proverbial driven snow. But thinking doesn't make it so."

Last night she'd acted so natural around Josh, he didn't believe she was pretending in order to impress Caige. Instead of revealing fear or revulsion of his son's condition, all he'd felt from her was compassion. She'd also looked a vision in that blue sweater.

"I've barely gotten beneath the surface, Mac." That was part of the problem. When he was with her, he forgot why he'd gone undercover. "Do me a favor and call this number?" He handed him a note. "Tell the manager at the Other Destinations travel agency I'll be around in fifteen minutes on official business." Caige shot to his feet. "Now I've got to run. See you later."

Before long, he entered the travel agency in question and told the man at the front desk he was there to see the manager. Caige was introduced to Mrs. Sanderson and followed her to her office.

"How can I help you, Ranger Dawson?"

"Your agency used to make airline arrangements for a Mr. Nathan Farley, who lived here in Austin with his wife, Blaire. He disappeared five years ago. I'm working on his case and need detailed information on all his transactions with your agency—airlines, hotels, rental cars, tickets for entertainment. Don't leave anything out. It could be of vital importance."

He wrote down his cell phone number and handed the note to her. "I'd appreciate it if you'd call me as soon as you can."

"Of course. I'll get right on it."

"Thank you."

On his way back to the restaurant to pick up Blaire, he stopped at Flowers by Phyllis. It was one of the shops on Farley's bank statement. Caige asked to talk to the business manager and was shown to an office at the rear of the busy store. After he'd displayed his ID and explained what he wanted, the manager assured him he'd find the information requested and get back to him.

Before Caige left, he bought two red poinsettias. The one for Elly he asked to be delivered. The other he was taking with him.

"Do you want me to wait with you?"

"Oh, no, Mom. You get back to your shopping. Jack will be along any minute." They'd just left the restaurant and were walking to her mother's car.

When they reached it, she gave Blaire a second look. "There's been something different about you all through lunch. What's going on?"

"What do you mean?"

"I don't know exactly. You seem…happier."

"Maybe that's because you've given me this new iPhone." She hugged her mom again. "Thank you for being so wonderful to me. How could I have lived through everything without you and Dad?" Visions of Jack having to carry the whole load with Josh weighed on her.

"Darling—what's brought this on?"

Blaire wiped her eyes. "Can't I tell my mom how much she means to me once in a while?"

Her mother smiled. "You tell me all the time, and the feeling's mutual." She got in her car.

Blaire shut the door. "I'll phone you tonight."

After watching her mother drive away, Blaire walked back to the sidewalk in front of the restaurant. Before long Jack's truck pulled up to the curb, and he opened the passenger door for her. By now she ought to be used to her heart doing a flip-flop at the sight of him. She jumped in and shut the door.

His eyes glanced at the bag she held. "What have you got in there?"

"My mom gave me my Christmas present early. It's the latest iPhone."

"Now, *that's* what I call a present. I couldn't live without mine. Have you experimented with it yet?"

She laughed. "All through lunch."

Jack reached for the iPhone in his breast pocket. "What's your number? I want to program it into my phone."

Her pulse sped up before she told him, "I'd like your number, too, but I don't know how to do that yet."

"Let me see yours and I'll fix it for you." Excited, she pulled out her new phone and handed it to him. "You go to favorites. Ah," he said, "it looks like I'll be the first one on your list." With a smile of satisfaction, he put in his number. "Now we don't have to go through Sheila."

He gave her back her phone, then put the truck in gear and they entered the stream of traffic. "Let's head for South River City since it's the farthest away."

"Good idea." She turned to him. "How was your lunch?"

"Nothing like yours, but a chili dog still gets the job done when you've got Christmas shopping to do."

"What did you buy?"

"For one thing, I went to a florist and had some flowers sent to my housekeeper. It's something she won't be expecting."

"Take it from me, she'll be thrilled."

"I hope so. Elly's a real treasure."

"How did you find her?"

"Through a friend at work. She told me this morning I'll be losing her next week."

"That's going to be hard on both you and Josh."

"The day had to come. Given time, I'll find someone else and the family will help."

Blaire bowed her head. Every time she thought about him moving to Naylor, she felt a deeper wrench. "What would we do without family? I was just telling my mother that before you drove up."

Jack flashed her a quick glance. "We're both lucky we never had to find out. Even so, you're a strong woman, Blaire. To live five years and still not know what happened to your spouse would bring most people to the breaking point."

She shook her head. "If anyone's remarkable, it's you. I don't know many men who would put their child before everything else. Josh is so sweet."

"My son didn't mind having you around last evening."

"How do you know that?"

"He didn't have a tantrum."

"I take it that's good," she teased.

"It's very good. Sometimes he'll just quit on you. Other times he bites or hits to get attention. I'm warning you now in case you'd like to come to my house on Friday night and decorate the tree with us. But if you have other plans, I understand, although I'll admit to being disappointed."

Jack had a way about him that filled her with excitement. To think that for the past four Christmases she'd stayed at her folks' to avoid doing anything to her own place because she couldn't bear the memories. Now suddenly there was nothing she wanted more than to be with Jack and help him make the holiday more meaningful for Josh.

"Well, I can't risk disappointing my colleague now, can I? So...I'd love to come."

"That's good because you didn't want to see *me* have a tantrum."

Unable to help it, she burst into laughter. But when she looked at him, all mirth subsided because tiny pinpoints of light shone through the beautiful gray of his irises, snatching her breath away.

For the rest of the afternoon they did their work climbing trees and taking samples while they talked their heads off about everything under the sun. After so many years of being alone, to be able to express her thoughts to someone as intelligent and fascinating as Jack Lignell was cathartic.

It was so much fun, she hated it to come to an end, but the second he took them back to the office, she knew he had to get home to Josh and couldn't linger. To her surprise, he drove her right over to her car. While she got behind the wheel, he pulled a wrapped floral gift from the bed of the truck and came around to put it on the floor of her front seat.

"What's this?"

He was leaning inside the car. Their gazes connected. "A small token for the way you handled Josh last night."

"But I didn't do anything—"

"That's the point. The few women I've taken around him freak out one way or another and he senses it. You're easy to be with, Blaire. See you in the morning." While her thoughts were spinning he added, "Are we supposed to wear our uniforms to the hotel for that presentation we're doing tomorrow?"

"Yes."

"Then I'll see you at eight." He shut the door and got back in the truck to park it with the others.

Blaire couldn't wait to get home. The second she entered her town house, she flew to the kitchen to undo the gift's outer wrapping. He'd gone to Flowers by Phyllis.

Nate had given her red roses from there both before and after they were married. She remembered because the name of the shop was distinctive, yet there was no stab of pain in the remembering. The memory didn't hurt anymore.…

After removing all the paper, she discovered a gorgeous red poinsettia with a red ribbon tied around the basket. A card had been inserted. With a trembling hand, she pulled it out of the little envelope. *You're one in a million. Jack.*

She read it over several times. "So are *you,*" she whispered and took the plant into the living room where she put it on her newly refinished coffee table.

This was her first Christmas decoration since becoming an unofficial widow. As of this moment, she decided that's what she was. In twenty-three more months, it would be official.

On a burst of adrenaline Blaire dashed back to the kitchen to get her new phone. She had to call him.

"Are you home safe?" his deep voice sounded after two rings.

"Safe, and delighted with the poinsettia. You shouldn't have done it, but I love it. Thank you, Jack."

"You're welcome."

"Are you home yet?"

"I'm just pulling in the driveway. I can see Josh looking out the living-room window. Elly always sits there on the couch with him when it's time for me to arrive."

Blaire's eyes smarted. "If she's already received her delivery, then she's probably as excited as he is. Thanks again for the beautiful plant. See you tomorrow."

THE AUSTIN REAL ESTATE Board, along with two hundred Realtors and land developers, had assembled in the downtown hotel conference room. Caige had scanned the list of attendees ahead of time on the off chance someone might be coming who would recognize him. To his relief, none of the names sounded familiar.

He knew Blaire had spoken to groups like this before and had everything under control. When she got up to address their audience, all eyes were on the stunning woman in uniform. Caige had a legitimate excuse to sit back and look at her all he wanted.

"Thank you for the introduction, Mr. Harris. My colleague and I are happy to be here today. In fact, we're eager for this opportunity because what we have to talk to you about is of vital importance to our community and state.

"Forgive me if I go over information you already know. What I'm going to ask is that you really think about the following things. Our intact forestlands supply timber products, wildlife habitat, soil and watershed protection, aesthetically beautiful scenery and recreational opportunities. As these areas become fragmented and disappear, so do the myriad benefits they provide.

"Our local governments can guide development away from the most sensitive areas through traditional land use tools such as zoning and performance standards, but sometimes these measures aren't sufficient to fully protect the forested component of our state's valuable natural-resource base. That's where the Forest Legacy Program comes in."

Caige felt her passion as she spoke. It infected him.

"This is a voluntary cooperative effort between the

USDA Forest Service and the State of Texas that protects ecologically important forests threatened by conversion to non-forest uses. The program encourages the voluntary protection of privately owned forestland. That's where you people come in. My colleague, Mr. Lignell, will explain further."

He could have listened to her speak indefinitely, but since she'd deferred to him, he had to get up and take the podium. Fortunately, he'd spent a lengthy time on the phone with Stan Belnap last night in order to be prepared for today's seminar.

"When you deal with a client, you need a thorough understanding of the acquisition of conservation easements. These are legally binding agreements transferring a negotiated set of property rights, primarily development rights, from one party to another without removing the property from private ownership.

"Most Forest Legacy Program conservation easements restrict development and require sustainable forestry practices. The USDA Forest Service State and Private Forestry branch administers the program in cooperation with the Texas Forest Service. It allows the state to purchase conservation easements on forestland with the goal of keeping the land in its forested state."

Caige looked over at Blaire. "If my colleague will come back to the podium, she'll tell you how it works." He knew he'd shocked her, but she handled it with grace, as she did everything else.

She cleared her throat. "Landowners may continue to own their land and retain all other rights to the property, including the right to sell the property. The conservation easement is recorded with the property deed and transferred with the sale or transfer of the property. For your information, the USDA Forest Service funds seventy-five percent of the easement purchase cost. The landowner provides twenty-five percent, and his or her share may come from nonfederal sources, such as a donation of part of the easement value from the landowner or a nonprofit organization interested in the project.

"We'll show a video and some slides to help further your understanding. Afterward, Mr. Lignell will entertain your questions."

"Touché," he whispered for her ears alone and was rewarded with a low chuckle.

Afterward, the seminar broke for lunch. When Mr. Harris invited them to eat at the table with the Real Estate Board, Caige excused himself for a minute and turned to Blaire. "I need to make a call, but I'll be right back." He'd just checked his phone messages. There was one from Gracie and another from the florist.

Once he'd found a place at the end of the hall where he had more privacy, Caige phoned the floral shop. "This is Ranger Dawson. You have information for me?"

"I found four orders for a dozen long-stemmed red roses sent within the time period you gave me. Three of them were charged to Mr. Farley's debit card and delivered to Blaire Farley on February 14, July 18 and November 10. The fourth order also went out on November 10 to Janie Pettigrew. That one was a cash payment."

Caige rubbed his jaw. *Cash?*

"Would you have any way of knowing if he phoned in those other orders?"

"No. I'm sorry."

That name was nowhere on the police record list of friends, colleagues or relatives of either Blaire or her husband. So who was she? Did it mean Farley didn't have enough money in his account at the time to charge both orders?

When Caige got back to his house, he'd look for the printout and see how much money had been sitting in there at the time the money was taken out for the November order.

"What's the address for the delivery to Janie Pettigrew?"

The florist gave him the address of the Sterling Luxury Condos in La Jolla, California.

"Were there messages with the flowers?"

"I'm afraid not. We're on a different computer system now."

"I see. That's fine. You've been a great help."

"Anytime."

He hung up and phoned Ernie. The older man told him he'd be faxing or emailing the picture of Farley and the artist's sketch of him to the various shooting ranges tomorrow morning.

"You do great work, Ernie. Now I need another favor."

"That's what I'm here for."

"Find out what you can on a Janie Pettigrew." He gave him her last known address in California. "Farley sent her *and* his wife a dozen red roses from the same florist five days before he disappeared, but he paid cash for the Pettigrew delivery. That's got me curious."

"Are you thinking she could be a family friend?"

"I don't know what I think."

"I'll check her out."

"Thanks."

Caige clicked off and listened to Gracie's message. She'd invited him and Josh for Sunday dinner. He sent her a message to tell her they'd be there and thanking her, then he hung up and joined Blaire, who was the center of attention at the table. No surprise there.

Her worried gaze flicked to him. "Is Josh all right?"

"As far as I know, he's fine."

"That's good."

His chicken entrée had been served. He sat down and started eating. Knowing she needed more of an explanation, he said, "I had a call from my friend Gracie. She asked Josh and me to dinner with her family on Sunday. Her daughters are really great with him. I needed to respond."

"How old are they?"

"Ten and twelve."

"Does Josh like them?"

"He smiles when they interact with him."

"I don't think he smiled at me the whole time we were playing golf."

"You don't give yourself enough credit. Have you forgotten he didn't have a meltdown with you?"

She reached for her coffee. "I guess that makes me feel a little better."

"It was supposed to," he murmured. "The girls have been playing with him for several years now."

Mr. Harris leaned forward to get Caige's attention. "I was just telling Ms. Koslov that your input at this seminar was invaluable. Everyone has come by the table expressing the same sentiment."

"Thank you." Caige eyed Blaire. "But she's the expert. I'm just filling in until her partner gets back from vacation in another week." Caige had anticipated the man asking them to speak to some other group. The less exposure he had in public, the better.

"Shall we go?" he asked her once they'd finished their dessert. "We've got four appointments this afternoon."

"I'm ready."

They said their goodbyes and walked through the hotel to the parking. Once they were back in the truck, she rested her head against the seat. "After that chocolate parfait, I'm so full I probably won't be able to climb any trees today."

"I'll help you up." He'd been waiting for the excuse to corner her in the branches of an oak. With a mass of leaves for a pillow, he'd kiss her mouth for as long as he wanted, showing no mercy. One day soon it was going to happen. But not before she knew the truth about him.

By the time he'd driven them back to the office at the end of the day, he'd made a decision. He wouldn't get physical with her until he could tell her he was Caige Dawson. That day would be here before he knew it because he still wasn't getting all the information he needed from her when they were together.

Blaire held the answers to too many questions, but to get them out of her meant interrogating her. In order to do that, he would have to tell her his real identity and explain that he'd been operating undercover to find out what had happened to her husband. After the trauma she'd lived through, she deserved all his honesty. Otherwise they couldn't hope to have a relationship if it turned out they both wanted one.

That was the other thing keeping him awake nights. Did he want to risk being in love a second time?

When he'd married Liz, he'd thought it was forever, that it would be his only relationship. When she had fallen apart after the accident, it had almost killed him. He'd believed she would eventually get back to her old self, but it hadn't happened. Her love for him hadn't been strong enough and it had finally killed his.

To start up a relationship with another woman meant beginning all over again. It meant going on faith, no matter what might be in store.

Caige was having a hard time separating the part of him heading this investigation from the man who was enjoying Blaire's company more and more. Was it Jack or Caige who'd invited her to go golfing?

Which man had invited her to help him trim the tree on Friday night? Which man was trying to find answers to the missing Nate Farley? Which man craved a more intimate association with her because he couldn't help himself?

If he knew the answers to those questions, would it even help? He closed his eyes tightly. With hindsight, he could see he shouldn't have told Mac he'd take on this case. The situation was playing games with his mind and his heart.

A shudder racked his body. There was only one thing he knew absolutely. Josh was his first priority.

He rubbed his eyes with the palms of his hands and took off for Modern Display. He'd seen an ad for a Santa with lights you could put up on the chimney. Caige didn't know if the decoration would even register with his son, but something his father had told him at Thanksgiving had stayed with him.

"One day in the hereafter when you're up there with your son talking man-to-man, I have a hunch he'll thank you for all the joy you brought to his life."

There was only one problem. Caige didn't want to have to wait that long for such a conversation.

In truth, he didn't want to go through the rest of this life without a companion. But if it was the wrong one for him, for Josh, Caige couldn't handle that.

THE SALESGIRL WALKED over to Blaire. "Hi. Can I help you find something?"

After driving away from the office, Blaire had come to Toy Castle and had been wandering around, but didn't know what to ask for. "You sell toys for handicapped children?"

"Yes."

"Oh, good. Josh is an eight-year-old who's brain-injured and doesn't talk, but he's active and goes to school. I'm going to be seeing him tomorrow night, and I wanted to take him a little present."

"Do you know if he has a pull ball?"

"I don't."

"They're very popular. Come over to the counter and I'll show you." She brought out a demonstrator yellow game, kind of like a small igloo cut in half. "This operates on two double-A batteries. It lights up and makes music when you gently tug on this tetherball. It will fly back inside when released."

Blaire tried it a few times. "I can see him liking the repetitive motion. I like this game myself." They both laughed. "I'll take it. Would you gift wrap it please?"

"Of course."

Maybe it wouldn't interest Josh, but she didn't want to arrive at Jack's house empty-handed. With her purchase in hand, Blaire left the store and drove to the mall to do some shopping for the family. She found a stunning red lapelled jacket and black pants for herself. Deciding to go all out, she bought a pair of black leather sandals with a medium heel.

Once back home, the first thing she saw when she entered her town house was the poinsettia. She would never see one again without thinking of Jack. He'd made her eager for Christmas to come. For everything!

She'd been positively giddy doing her job with him this afternoon. He was amazingly well-informed and knew more political jokes than she could believe. It seemed they had the same slant when it came to politics, a subject she normally couldn't discuss with many people.

Blaire wished they were going out tonight, yet the minute she entertained the thought, she realized she was out of control. That's what came from being a widow for five years. Somehow she needed to find a way to slow down.

But how to do that when she'd spent time with Jack, the most…oh, she couldn't even find the words for the way he made her feel. He was like this fabulous mosaic of so many textures and colors, she wouldn't know where to begin describing him.

Today he'd had the Realtors eating out of his hand. He had sophistication. His wealth of knowledge astounded her. The man could tackle any subject. Sometimes he was funny, other times serious, tender, kind. He was the best listener she'd ever known. There was no end to the list of his outstanding traits. She found him without flaw, inside or out.

Easy, easy, Blaire! There was no such animal.

That was a dangerous kind of talk that could only get her into trouble.

She already *was* in trouble.

When the phone rang and she saw the name on the caller ID, heat swarmed her cheeks. After four rings she clicked on. "Hello?"

"Hi. Did I catch you at the wrong moment?"

"No." She sank down on the side of her bed. "But my phone was on the other side of the room."

"Mine's usually in the wrong place, too."

"Is everything all right with Josh?"

"Yes. At the moment he's turning my bedroom light switch off and on. He loves to do that. It's a good thing I can handle flashing lights since he sometimes keeps it up for ten minutes at a time."

Blaire chuckled softly. "After listening to you deal

with all the questions at the seminar, I've a feeling you can handle anything."

"It would be nice if it were true. The reason I'm calling is to find out what you'd like for dinner tomorrow. I'm leaving for the store in a few minutes. It'll be Elly's night off, so I'll be doing the cooking. You have three choices."

She smiled to herself. "What does Josh like?"

"Pancakes."

"Can we have those? I love them, especially when they're not for breakfast."

There was a brief silence. "Well, that was so easy I guess I don't need to go anywhere."

"After the hard day we put in, I'd stay put if I were you. I'll write up our notes on my computer. See you in the morning."

"Blaire?" Some nuance in his voice drew her attention.

"Yes?"

"On second thought, nothing. It'll keep until tomorrow."

"Nope. You can't do that to me. Tell me what's on your mind."

"How did you happen to become a plant pathologist?"

"You want to know that *now?* After we've been climbing trees all afternoon? That's not what you were going to ask me."

He laughed. "Even so, I still want to know."

"Well, I always loved music. When I went to college, I intended to become a music major in the performance end of it. But I also loved the biological sciences and took a botany class. After looking in the microscope, I was snagged."

"I guess we have that in common."

"I don't know if you ever saw the old film classic about Louis Pasteur, but when I watched it, I fell in love with the idea of what you could see when you looked through the lens. It decided me on a career and I changed majors, which took me a little more time to graduate." She smiled to herself. "How did *you* happen to end up working for the forest service?"

"I was a rancher first and loved the land, but wanted to learn more. In college several opportunities opened up, but I soon realized I needed to work in the outdoors as much as possible. I like being free. If I had to sit in an office all day, I couldn't do it."

"Neither could I." She got to her feet. "Now tell me what you were originally going to ask me."

"I'm afraid it's a sensitive subject. I've hesitated broaching it in case it sounded like I was prying."

"You mean Nate."

"Yes. I realize it's still painful for you, but I've been wondering what drew you together, how you met. Do you mind my wanting to know?" he asked in a more serious tone.

She gripped the phone tighter. "Jack—you need to understand something. He's been gone too long for it to be painful anymore. For the first few years it was the *not* knowing what happened to him that made it so hard, but I'm over that."

"I'm glad for you," he whispered.

Now that she'd told him this much, she might as well go all the way. "As for how we met, I used to go to the football games when I was in college. One day Nate sat behind me and my girlfriends. We got talking and—"

"And that was it," he finished the sentence for her. "Thank you for helping me put all the pieces together."

"Pieces?"

"I've been trying to fit the various parts of you into a whole that makes you, you."

"I guess we've both been doing that, so maybe you won't mind if I ask you the same question. How did you meet the woman who gave you such a beautiful son?" Blaire had wanted to know, but had been afraid to bring it up. Now was her opportunity to do so without seeming to be too curious.

"Liz sideswiped my empty car by accident while she was backing out of her parking spot at the movies."

"Oh, dear."

"To her credit, she left a note on my windshield with her name and phone number for the insurance exchange."

Blaire bit her lip, imagining it was love at first sight for them. "Before you knew anything else about her, you learned she was honest. Besides being kind, I think that's one of the most important things you can know about a person."

"I agree." He took a long time before he said, "Blaire—before we hang up, I wanted you to know I have a business appointment in the morning. I'll call you when I'm finished so you can tell me where to find you."

Her heart sank, silly girl. "Oh. That's fine."

"When you're ready to take your lunch break, I'll work through it to make up my time. Tomorrow night we'll forget live oak wilt and play."

"I'm looking forward to it. Good night." She hung up quickly before she was tempted to tell him she couldn't wait.

Chapter Five

Sixty-two degrees and holding. The weather couldn't be better for Caige, who was up on the roof attaching Santa to the chimney. He'd already dropped off Josh at school and had been to court to testify at the nine o'clock hearing for the felon he'd brought in last month.

Now he could take his time to do this right before he joined Blaire. He was just attaching the last clamp when his cell phone went off. It would have to ring until he'd finished the job.

A few minutes later it was done. If he said so himself, the Santa would be able to withstand some wind. Before climbing down, he reached in his pocket for the phone and discovered Ernie had left a message. Instead of listening to it, he called him. "Morning, Ernie. What's up?"

"Not much yet. No one named Janie Pettigrew is living at the Sterling Condos now. New management took over last year. I phoned the person you need to talk to from the old management, but he's out of town until next Wednesday. The info is on the message I left with you.

"In case she was a student here, if only for a few

semesters, I phoned the UT Austin campus admissions office. They wouldn't give me any information without a search warrant so I called the judge. He'll issue you one, but if you need it soon, you have to get over there pronto. At lunch he's leaving town for ten days."

Caige had just been to the court building. "Call him back and tell him I'm coming now. Have his secretary put the time on the warrant between ten and eleven o'clock." He was going to be later than he'd thought to catch up to Blaire, but now was his chance to find out what he could.

"Will do."

"Thanks, Ernie."

"You bet. Before you hang up, you need to know I phoned Motor Vehicles. They checked ten years back to the present and found no person with that exact name driving a car or a boat with a Texas license plate. However, there were hundreds of derivatives."

Naturally. "What about rental-car agencies?"

"I'm working on those now. Then I'll get busy looking for her in the California DMV database."

"When you're always a step ahead of me, I don't know why I asked. Talk to you later."

The man was pure gold.

Caige put the ladder away and took off for the municipal court building to pick up the warrant. With it in hand, he was able to sit down with one of the registrars on campus. In case this Janie was a friend of the Farleys, he asked the woman to go back ten years and start through the Pettigrews.

Everything from Jan to Jane to Janet to Janeal to

Jayna and Jeanette came up. For all he knew they could all have Janie for a nickname. He came across initials like J. B. and J. C. Pettigrew, but they turned out to be males.

One J. J. Pettigrew caught his eye because it was a female. He jotted down the local phone number listed in case it was still a working number, then thanked the registrar and went out to the car to call Blaire.

He got her voice mail. It meant she was probably performing surgery on a tree, so he phoned Sheila who gave him addresses for the next scheduled appointments. Before he drove off, he tried the phone number he'd taken from the student file, but it belonged to Biffy's Car Wash, one of a chain throughout the state.

Caige would ask Ernie to call the phone company and find out the full name of the person who'd had the phone number before it was assigned to Biffy's.

Instead of driving to the office for the truck he'd been issued, he headed for the nearest address Sheila had given him. He saw Blaire's truck parked at the side of the street. When he found her, she was talking to the woman who lived there.

Blaire acknowledged him with a smile. "Mr. Lignell? This is Mrs. Wiseman. I've inspected this Texas ash and was telling her the reason for the curled leaves is aphids." She held up some foliage to show the dense cluster of insects. "They're most prevalent in spring and fall, but they can be managed with chemical control."

"Where should I call?"

Caige pulled a card out of his pocket. "The person

who answers will give you a list of a dozen places for pest control."

"Thank you."

"If you get right on it, you'll be able to save your tree," Blaire assured her.

"I'll phone them in a few minutes."

They said goodbye and Caige walked Blaire to the truck. "Sorry I'm late again, but it couldn't be helped."

"You don't need to explain." She climbed in her truck and shut the door.

"Anyone can see you don't need a partner."

She stared straight at him. "Are you trying to tell me something?"

"That I'm impressed with your expertise? Yes."

Her blue eyes danced. "Thank you. Coming from a Trees for Texas man, that's high praise."

"Only because it's the truth. I'll follow you to our next appointment."

"We only have two more. Drive safely," she reminded him this time before pulling away.

He got in his car and started after her, thinking about their conversation last night. It had illuminated his need to come clean with her before much more time passed. He'd already accomplished his first objective and knew without a doubt she was not involved with her husband's disappearance. There was no more necessity for him to stay undercover.

But he also recognized that once he removed the mask, the magic between them would disappear and her defenses would go up. That was the downside of deception, even when it was for the purest of reasons.

Caige had to admit that during this week, he'd experienced a kind of happiness he hadn't thought could come again in this life. This morning he'd sprung out of his bed to take his shower because he knew he'd be seeing her in a few hours.

Instead of the novelty wearing off because they worked together all day long, the opposite had happened and he found she was growing on him. He never got tired of her. It was getting harder and harder to say goodbye after they drove back to the office. At least tonight she'd be coming over to his house. He was living for it.

En route to their next appointment he received a call from Other Destinations.

"Ranger Dawson? This is Mrs. Sanderson."

"Yes. Were you able to retrieve the information?"

"Yes. I'll give you what I've found for the time period you gave me."

"I need to write it down, but I'm in my car. May I call you back in a few minutes?"

"Of course."

"Thank you."

Caige kept following Blaire, who eventually pulled up in front of a residence with a half-dozen black walnut trees. He could tell that two of them were in trouble. He parked behind her and called out the window that he had an important call and would catch up with her. She nodded and went up to the front door of the house.

He drew the small notepad from his pocket before returning the phone call. "Hi. This is Ranger Dawson. Go ahead and give me the information."

"For the months in question, there are twelve round-trips from Austin to San Diego. All are mix-and-match weekend lower fares." The woman listed the dates.

"For two people?"

"No. One person."

"The name of the passenger on the tickets?"

"Nathan Farley." Twelve trips without Blaire?

"Any hotels, rental cars?"

"No, sir."

"Thank you very much."

By the time he was ready to join Blaire, she'd already diagnosed the trees with walnut blight. She told the owners that the affected parts had to be burned to save the trees. After explaining how to accomplish the procedure, they took off for their last appointment.

An older man at the next house was upset because the red oaks in his front yard were suffering from oak decline and would need injections of fungicide in June to save them. Blaire explained the problem in such a way that she managed to reassure him he wouldn't lose his trees if he followed her instructions.

Caige gave the man a card that would help him find a company to come out and do an expert job. They chatted quietly for a few minutes before saying goodbye.

"I've told you before," he said as he helped Blaire back in her truck. "You remind me of a highly skilled surgeon with an impressive treeside manner, Dr. Koslov."

She scoffed at his comment, but color tinted her cheeks. "What time do you want me to make a house call tonight, Mr. Lignell?"

He studied her lovely features. The pulse at her throat throbbed noticeably. "As soon as you can get ready and come over. Here's my address." He wrote it on a piece of paper from his notepad and handed it to her. "I only live three miles from the office. My house will be the only one on the street with a red Toyota in the driveway."

"I'll find you."

Two hours later Blaire turned onto the street where Jack lived in the Crestview area of north-central Austin. During the drive from her town house, dusk had melted into darkness. Most of the ranch-style houses in his neighborhood were already decorated, but only one had a bigger-than-life Santa lit up on the roof.

While she marveled at the brave soul who'd put it up there, she realized it was Jack's house because she saw his car. He'd left the porch light on for her. A lighted Christmas tree glowed from the front window. After she'd parked behind the Toyota, she reached for the gift she'd brought for Josh and, with a pounding heart, hurried up to the front door. Before she could ring the bell, it opened.

The dangerously dark and handsome man standing in the shadows of the dimly lit foyer was a new version of her temporary coworker. All the tough lines and angles of his face and body were highlighted like the relief on a coin. For some reason he seemed taller without his uniform. Over tan chinos he wore a black long-sleeved crewneck sweater that looked like cashmere. Casual yet elegant.

Blaire felt his gaze taking her in. "You look stunning."

"So do you, Jack Lignell," she answered boldly. "They say a uniform does something for a person, but I have to admit it's nice to see you in different attire. It brings out the mysterious in you." She saw something flicker in the gray eyes smiling at her. An odd feeling stole through her she couldn't account for.

"Josh and I are glad you're here. Come in."

Though it was chillier outside now, she hadn't worn a coat. It was just as well because a fire blazed inside her. After closing the front door, he showed her through some French doors to the living room with its traditional decor and feel. His ex-wife's influence?

He'd put some decorations on the mantel and coffee table, but the tree needed ornaments. "Everything looks beautiful. You chose a noble fir, my favorite kind." She leaned down to put her present on the skirt beneath the limbs.

"Mine, too, obviously." His voice sounded deeper than usual.

"Where's Josh?" She raised up to look at him once more. It was hard to do anything but stare when he was so striking.

"In the kitchen playing with some of the pots and pans. He likes to do that when I cook."

"You're not dressed for making pancakes."

"A little flour never hurt anything."

"You're right. Do you think he'll remember me?"

"I don't know. Let's find out. After we eat, we'll

come back in here to decorate the tree. I would have started a fire, but it's not that cold out tonight."

"You're right."

She followed him back into the foyer and through the opposite set of doors to the formal French-provincial dining room. Another door led to the charming kitchen dominated by an oval table and chairs. It was set for three. The feminine touches throughout the interior reminded her another woman had once lived in this house.

But when she saw Jack tousle his son's hair while he sat on the floor, bringing a smile to his precious face, she realized this man was the heart and soul of this home. "Look who's here, buddy. We've got a visitor."

Blaire drew closer. "Hi, Josh. Those pans are fun, aren't they?"

The boy kept playing with the gadgets and pots his father had put out for him. She flicked Jack a glance. "While you cook, I've got an idea. I'll be right back." In another minute she had brought her gift into the kitchen and put it down on the floor by Josh.

He didn't seem to notice, so she undid the wrapping and drew the pull-ball game out of the box. When she started to play with it, he watched the tetherball go in and out. Now that it made music and she had his attention, she put it up on the table.

To her delight he got up from the floor and came over to see it. He wanted to do it and took over. Blaire sank down on a chair to watch him. At one point he smiled. It matched the broad one on Jack's arresting male features.

Jack brought hotcakes and sausage to the table. The

two of them ate and drank coffee while Josh continued to play. "You like that, buddy?"

Josh hadn't touched his pancakes yet. He just smiled again. This time she thought it might have included her.

She leaned toward Jack. "There are extra batteries in the box in case you need them."

"At this rate I'm pretty sure we'll be putting more in before the night is out. That's a winner toy if I ever saw one." With those words, he devoured two more pancakes in a couple of swallows.

"I remember what you said about him liking to turn the light switch on and off. The salesgirl said it was a popular item."

He studied her over the rim of his coffee cup. "You're something else, you know that?"

"Because I brought a little toy to a boy for Christmas?"

"Because of that, and everything else that went with it. The thought, the caring."

"It's long past time I thought about someone else besides myself. You've had to forget yourself for so long, I feel ashamed. Meeting you has caused me to turn over a new leaf. Even though it's not New Year's, I've made a resolution to enjoy every minute of the rest of my life and never look back again."

"Everyone should adopt such a resolution. The world would be a much happier place."

"Every child should have a daddy like you. I saw that Santa up on your housetop. Has Josh seen it lit up?"

Jack had been lounging back in the chair, studying her through veiled eyes. "Not yet."

"After I help you do the dishes, let's take him outside to look at it."

"The dishes can wait. I'll grab his parka."

Jack got up from the table and left the kitchen. Josh didn't seem bothered, but when his father returned, it was as if he'd just noticed he was gone and ran over to him. "Come on, buddy." He put the coat on his boy. "We're going to go outside for a minute."

He held Josh's hand and the three of them walked through the house. When they got out in the air, Jack moved to the end of the driveway so they could get the full effect.

"Look, Josh—" Blaire pointed to the chimney. "That's Santa Claus!"

Maybe it was meaningless to him. She couldn't tell. Jack lifted the child in his arms and pointed. Josh imitated his father by lifting his free arm. He must have thought it was a game. If so, it was endearing.

She started singing in a quiet voice. "Up on the housetop the reindeer pause, out jumps dear old Santa Claus—"

Josh's head suddenly swung around. He stared straight at her while she went on singing. Jack joined in. It brought a smile to Josh's face before he kissed his daddy's cheek half a dozen times.

"With kisses like that, I'd say you've made your son pretty happy, Jack."

She started back into the house ahead of them because she was afraid she couldn't hold back her tears. By the time Jack and Josh entered the kitchen, she'd cleared the table and was putting dishes in the dishwasher.

"Leave it and come with me. We've got a tree to decorate." But Josh didn't want to go without his pull ball. Clutching it in his arms, he followed his father into the living room.

While Josh played on the floor with his new toy, Blaire helped put elves and red satin balls on the tree.

"All finished," Jack said at last. When he turned in her direction, the look he gave her left her feeling light-headed. "If the star weren't already on top, I'd put you up there. You brought magic into this house tonight."

Before she could think, he pressed a brief kiss to her lips. "Merry Christmas, Blaire Koslov. My son thanks you for the gift. Now it's time for him to go to bed. I won't be long."

After he'd left the room, she still felt the pressure of his mouth against hers. The moment was one she was destined to relive because she feared she'd fallen in love with him. Of course, you couldn't really fall in love with someone this fast, but she couldn't attribute this feeling to anything else.

Maybe it would be better if she made this an early evening so he wouldn't think she was expecting more from him. The kiss he'd given her had suited the moment. She knew he was grateful for any help with his son.

Since there was still next week to get through before Perry returned to work, the smart thing to do would be to keep their relationship uncomplicated. That meant no physical intimacy. Another week working side by side with him and they'd both know their feelings better.

Once they weren't colleagues any longer, she'd welcome a night like this alone with him.

Rather than sit here, she decided to make herself useful until he was free.

Chapter Six

You couldn't hurry the bedtime ritual with Josh, but Caige wasn't worried. Eager as he was to be alone with Blaire, he knew that when he returned to the living room, he wouldn't find her put out because he'd been gone ten minutes. This woman was the opposite of high maintenance.

Her nonintrusive nature hadn't disturbed the rhythm of his relationship with his son. If anything, her presence had acted as a soothing balm. It was the reason Josh fell asleep right away.

He kissed his boy good-night before heading for the living room. When he didn't see Blaire, he made a detour to the kitchen and found her at the table drinking more coffee. She'd put the place in perfect order. "I didn't invite you over here to work."

"I know, but now you don't have to worry about it, or Elly. It gave me something to do. I take it Josh is asleep."

"If he weren't, we'd both know about it." Caige poured himself a cup of coffee and sat down opposite her, the better to feast his eyes. She was gorgeous in red.

"Your home is lovely, Jack. Did you always live here with your wife?"

"Yes. After we divorced I wanted to sell this place and get into something new, but I was afraid to move Josh away from everything familiar. The doctor felt it wisest if I didn't change the life he was used to, so I took his advice."

"I got the opposite advice." She laughed at herself. "In the beginning I didn't want to leave our apartment because—"

"Because you hoped he'd open the door and walk in one of these days," he broke in on her. "That was only natural."

"My brother, Mark, didn't think so. He said it was gruesome of me to sit around waiting."

"He's never been married, right?"

"No." She lowered her head. "In the end he was the one who told me I had to get out and convinced me to go on to graduate school. My psychiatrist agreed with him. So with my family's backing, he helped me find an apartment in College Station. Mark was excellent medicine, but it didn't feel that way at the time."

"He sounds like a man I'd like."

"You two would hit it off big-time. He's a motorcycle lover, too, and bought his first one when he was seventeen. His prized Kawasaki is stored in my parents' garage right now."

"Did he ever take you for a ride?"

"Quite a few times, but our parents have never been thrilled by the idea."

"Did you like it?"

"I loved it."

"You say your brother's in the navy. Where's he stationed?"

"San Diego."

"Have you ever been there?"

She nodded. "On family vacations."

"It's a romantic place. Liz and I went there several times. What about you and your husband?"

"After our honeymoon to Maui, we didn't travel. All our extra money went to private golf lessons for Nate so he could turn pro sooner."

"I thought he'd worked out a deal with Danny Dunn."

"He did. I'm talking about the lessons he took in San Diego. We had to save every cent for them. It's odd you would mention San Diego just now. Once a month he flew down there to get expert instruction at the Torrey Pines golf course. Mr. Dunn arranged it with one of his pro golfer friends who'd retired and ran the program."

"Who was that?"

"Tally Isom. He won several PGA championships during his career. Apparently Mr. Dunn got his start with him."

Caige rubbed the back of his neck. "That was a fortunate connection. What did you do on those weekends?"

"I studied extra hard and held recitals at the apartment for my students."

She hadn't balked at all his questions yet, but if he didn't stop interrogating her, she was going to ask what was going on. The problem was, he still had a ton of them and needed tomorrow to dot a few more *i*'s before he told her who he was. As for right now, what he wanted to do with her he couldn't do, not when she didn't know the whole truth about him.

If Elly were here, he could leave and take Blaire to a film or something. It was only five after ten. When he'd invited her over tonight, he hadn't anticipated boxing himself into a corner like this. He hadn't known how cooperative Josh would be. "How would you like to go in the den and watch a movie?"

"I'd love it, but while you were in with Josh, Gwen phoned. She reminded me I'd promised to tend her baby in the morning while she took her car in to be serviced. I have to be at her house at seven, so I think I'd better say good-night and get home to bed." Without hesitation she got to her feet.

Blaire was lying, otherwise she would have told him as soon as he'd come in the kitchen. He shouldn't have kissed her, even if they'd both wanted it. In his gut he knew she wanted him. Desire wasn't something you could hide. But because he hadn't been able to keep himself from touching her, that one unsatisfying peck for him had altered the situation before time. *Damn*.

"If you're really ready to go home, then I'll walk you out."

"Breakfast was delicious," she said as they left the house and moved to her car. "I had a wonderful time."

"So did I." He helped her in. "Take care driving home. Do you have to park outside?"

"No. I have a garage."

"That's good. When you're inside, give me a call to let me know you arrived."

"I will. Thanks again for the lovely evening, Jack.

See you on Monday morning." She backed out and drove away.

He wanted to see her sooner, but he had a full weekend planned to work on her case, plus dinner at Gracie's. Depending on circumstances, it might have to be Monday.

Caige turned off the lights on the Santa and the tree, then locked up the house and went to his den. To work off his excess energy, he sat down and called information for numbers he would need. In the morning while Elly fixed Josh's breakfast, he would start making phone calls.

Blaire's input, combined with the dates from the travel agency records, gave him the rudiments of a map to follow, the first of many he feared might not lead anywhere. It was like looking for buried treasure without X marking the spot. There were no directions. Two paces in this direction. Ten paces in the next. It was all a gamble.

He rubbed his eyes. A week ago he'd made a list of possibilities and would keep working it until he got a break in the case. So far there were two things he knew. Blaire was innocent of any crime *and* she'd become a person of personal interest to him. As if thinking about her had conjured her up, his phone rang, causing a burst of adrenaline. He saw the caller ID and answered.

"Are you home safe and sound?"

"I'm in the living room turning out lights as we speak. The poinsettia you gave me is flourishing."

"This morning Elly told me hers is, too. She's keeping it in her bedroom."

"A woman loves her flowers. I thought you should be told. When you order them over the phone, you don't always know if they arrived in the peak of health."

"So speaks our resident pathologist. I'll have to let the florist know."

"You do that. Good night."

She got off the phone so fast, he felt like someone had just cut the tether. He was left to float in the same void where he'd been floundering before Blaire had jumped down from that oak tree.

He finally went to bed, but didn't sleep well. At six, he was wide-awake. Unable to lie there any longer, he showered and dressed. Unfortunately, the people he needed to talk to were in California and wouldn't be available yet, but Josh was awake.

The two of them went in the living room where Josh found the pull ball. Jack played with his son until Elly called them to breakfast. By the time he'd had a second bowl of cereal with bananas, he figured he could start making a dent in the work ahead of him. After bringing in some of Josh's toys while Elly did her chores, he left for his den and called Torrey Pines first.

According to the website, it was the nation's premier municipal golf course, overlooking the Pacific Ocean and home to the PGA Farmers Insurance Open.

After telling the receptionist this was official police business, he asked to be put through to the manager. Caige didn't expect the manager to be in on a Saturday morning, but someone else with lesser authority ought to be able to help him.

"This is Arney King, the assistant manager." Assistant would do. "Who am I speaking to?"

"Caige Dawson of the Texas Rangers in Austin, Texas." Caige gave him his ID number and a phone number so he could call for verification. "I'm working on a missing-person case and need certain information."

"I'll try to be of help."

"Thank you." For the next few minutes he gave him the necessary particulars. "Could you look up the dates I've given you and see if Nathan Farley paid the fees and attended those Saturday golf sessions with Tally Isom?"

"That'll take some time to research."

"Of course. Does Mr. Isom still head the program?"

"No. About a year ago he had a stroke. I believe his family put him in a rest home."

"Do you know which one?"

"I don't, but I'll inquire and call you back with everything I can find."

Caige thanked him. Once they'd hung up, he went to his emails. He had at least twenty-five. Some from family, the others were business. He saw Ernie's and opened his first. The older man had forwarded him the information from the California DMV on Janie Pettigrews in San Diego County. There were thirty-two of them. Ernie indicated he'd already started working on them.

Another email came from Mac, who'd talked with the detective heading up the investigation of the Dunn murder. They were working on the new lead Blaire had given Caige about the caddy named Ron. Mac would get back to him when he had any news.

With everyone involved, it was still like looking for a certain snake in a pit of thousands.

He read the family emails. His parents wanted to know how soon he and Josh were coming for Christmas. Good question. Caige said he'd get back to them in another few days.

While he waited to hear from Mr. King, he started going through the debits on Farley's bank statements. He checked the florist's statement again. There'd been over five hundred dollars in the account when he'd charged the flowers sent out in November. That meant he'd paid cash for the other flowers for a specific reason, not because he was low on money. Interesting...

Farley wasn't a big spender or extravagant. Their grocery buying was in control. A few purchases for movie tickets, a couple of items from a department store and one from a photography studio.

It looked like they ate out once a month at restaurants with moderate prices, a few drive-in charges. They weren't buying anything on credit except their lower-end economy cars. No excessive gas purchases. Since Farley worked in a bank and needed to wear a suit, there were charges from a local cleaning shop that made sense. But a lot of things Caige might have expected to see weren't there.

Except for the flights to California once a month, he and Blaire were frugal where their expenditures were concerned. If every couple managed their money in the same way, people wouldn't be in debt. Farley was so temperate in his spending habits, he could be one of those souls who had Scottish blood in him and came by his financial discipline naturally.

But there was one thing wrong with that picture— Farley had dreamed of becoming a pro golfer from his teens. Everything about the game was expensive and screamed money. It meant he must have had another source of income somewhere to support that lifestyle— one he'd taken the greatest pains to hide.

The cash he'd paid for the flowers was a little thing in and of itself, but those flowers had gone to someone else, not his wife. Cash meant you didn't leave a paper trail. Farley's association with Danny Dunn had begun long before he'd met Blaire. It could have opened up a way for him to have money his wife had no clue about.

If Farley was right and Dunn's professional caddy was his lover, maybe this Ron was jealous of Farley's association with Dunn. Maybe Farley had purchased his gun for protection. But it had done him little good if Ron had found a way to get rid of Farley after killing Dunn.

Caige rubbed the back of his neck, frustrated because all this was pure conjecture. He could be way off base with his ideas. It had happened before in other cases. It could be happening now. Without the vital missing piece to link it all together, he didn't—

The phone interrupted his thoughts. He automatically clicked on. "This is Ranger Dawson."

"Arney King here. Sorry it took me so long. I talked with the head of the program just now. He went through all the records for the time periods you gave me. No one named Nathan Farley from Austin, Texas, ever signed up for lessons at Torrey Pines. The finance department verified that his name isn't in their records."

Caige shot out of his chair and paced the floor for a second to calm down. "Did you happen to find out the name of that convalescent center where Tally Isom was admitted?"

"Yes. It's the North Shady Pines in Fresno, California."

"Thank you for the information. It's been invaluable."

Caige hung up and reached for Josh, who'd come in the den to play by him. He lifted him in the air. "Guess what, buddy? I'm getting closer to solving this case. You have no idea what this means to me." He sat down again with Josh on his lap and called information for Fresno.

While his son played with the kinetic-motion desk toy Caige's sister had given him years ago, he talked to the woman in charge of the center and explained the situation. She told him the stroke had taken away Mr. Isom's ability to speak or walk, and had left him confused. It didn't sound as if he'd be able to identify a picture in case Farley had registered under another name for some reason.

Caige thanked her for the information and rang off. He rested his chin in Josh's hair while his mind played with new possibilities. What if Farley had been a wannabee pro who knew he wasn't good enough?

If he hadn't gone to California for golf lessons, then he could have been over his head in some gambling scheme with Dunn. He probably had money in an account in California under a different name so no one would ever find out, especially not his wife.

When he thought about her and the sacrifices she'd made to help him achieve his dream—totally unaware of her husband's lie—his gut turned in rage.

"Come on, buddy. We're going for a ride to Naylor." Caige did some of his best thinking while he was driving to see his family.

WHEN BLAIRE WALKED INTO the office Monday morning, Jack was already there working on their schedule for the day. His gaze shot to hers before he said good morning. He sounded more sober than usual.

She'd spent a wretched weekend wishing she'd stayed at his house to watch a movie with him. Instead she'd run off because of her fears and insecurities. Worse, she'd given him an excuse for leaving that a ten-year-old would have seen through.

Today she was desperate to repair any damage she'd caused because she didn't want to lose Jack. After greeting everyone, she walked over to his desk. "How was dinner at your friend Gracie's house?"

"We had a terrific time. What about you?" His gray eyes seemed to penetrate hers. "Did your sister get her car serviced?"

"No, but I'll tell you about that after we're on our way. Have you finished?"

"I have one more appointment to make."

"How's it going, Blaire?" Marty had just come in.

She glanced over at him. "Things are great. Did you get that kiln for your wife?"

"They promised to deliver it by the twenty-third."

"I hope so. It will make her Christmas. She's a real artist. I love that plate she made me. With you giving her a gift like that, she'll probably let you watch at least one football game Christmas day."

Marty chuckled. "Are you ready for the big event?"

"Pretty much." After the way Josh had responded to his pull-ball toy, she knew what other gifts to buy for him. As for Jack, she hadn't decided yet. Something that wasn't personal. Maybe a DVD about a dog he could watch with his son.

"Shall we go?" Jack had finished and put a copy of their schedule in Sheila's basket. He definitely had something on his mind.

"I'm ready. See you guys later." They walked out of the building.

"It's my turn to drive," he asserted, almost as if he expected an argument. She didn't give him one and climbed in the cab once he'd unlocked the doors. This was a new side to Jack. If her behavior Friday night had anything to do with it, then she wanted to clear the air.

"How's that darling boy of yours?"

"Good. On Saturday we drove to Naylor so he could play with his cousins."

That wasn't the only reason Jack had gone there, but she didn't want to hear that he'd found some property to buy and had a date in mind for his big move from Austin.

"About Saturday morning—" she began. "I'm afraid I have a confession to make."

"You mean your sister didn't need you at seven o'clock in the morning. I figured that out or you would have said something earlier."

Nothing got past Jack. He had a brilliant mind. "Forgive me for lying to you. I hate lies," she whispered.

"So do I, but sometimes they're necessary."

She bit her lip. "They're never necessary, but they're easy to fall back on if you're not secure enough in your own skin to face the truth."

"What truth can't you face?" He sure didn't mince words.

Blaire swallowed hard. "You're too intelligent a man not to know."

"You're talking about the attraction between us. It's real, all right. As long as we're talking truth here, I have a confession of my own to make."

Uh-oh. She couldn't imagine what was coming, unless this had something to do with his ex-wife. Maybe she was divorcing her second husband because she wanted Jack and Josh back. Blaire still couldn't comprehend a woman, no matter how deep her pain, who would willingly leave Jack.

If he could have her back, it might explain why he hadn't crushed Blaire in his arms the other night the way she'd wanted him to do. "Go ahead and tell me."

She heard a sharp intake of breath. "Our first appointment is only two blocks away. After we've finished, I'll drive us to a park where we can talk. I spaced our next appointment to allow us the time."

He needed *that* kind of time? This sounded even more serious and troubling.

Blaire was thankful for another oak wilt problem at the next address. Climbing trees helped her work off her angst about what was coming. No more chatting or laughter while they took samples. Something was terribly wrong. She had a foreboding.

After they'd gone back to the truck with the ice chest and had pulled away from the curb, she turned to him because she had a sick feeling in the pit of her stomach. "Why don't you just tell me now and get it over with."

"The park is only a few minutes away."

They were the longest minutes she'd ever known. Eventually they wound around to a grassy area some distance away from a playground. He shut off the motor.

"Please say what's on your mind."

He angled his hard-muscled body toward her. "As I told you earlier, sometimes lies are necessary."

"You mean in certain lines of work, like counter-intelligence."

He nodded his dark head. "That's one example."

"Are you about to tell me you're a former espionage agent for the military or some such thing?" He had the intelligence and instincts to be one.

"Not exactly." He reached in his back pocket and pulled an item from his wallet before handing it to her.

Blaire recognized the circle-in-the-star badge right away. *Captain* was inscribed in the center. The blood in her body suddenly congealed to ice. "You're a Texas Ranger," she whispered.

His silence condemned him.

She turned on him. "You've been investigating me all this time?" she cried in anguish. White-hot pain caused her to throw his badge at him before she got out of the truck and started running.

"Blaire, wait—" She knew he was coming after her. On those long, powerful legs of his, he'd reach her before she had a chance to get away.

There was a stand of live oaks on the other side of the playground. Instinct drove her to head there where she climbed the first one. Quickly she scrambled up the branches into the top part of the old tree. Just as fast, Jack caught up to her until they faced each other with only inches to spare. His skin had a pallor that hadn't been noticeable earlier.

"Well, you've got me trapped." Her breathing was so shallow, she could hardly talk. "What happened, *Ranger* Lignell? Did my husband's body turn up? Is that what this is all about? Are you planning to arrest me for his murder?"

His gorgeous gray eyes looked tormented, but they couldn't match the torment she was feeling. "There's no body yet, alive or dead. Two weeks ago your parents approached FBI Agent Tim Robbins, hoping he could do something about your case."

Angry tears filled her eyes. "My *parents* know about this?"

"Only in the sense that Robbins told them he'd see what he could do. He doesn't work for the FBI in Austin anymore, so he approached my superior, Mac Leesom. He in turn came to me and asked me to work on your case as a personal favor to him."

Surely this was a nightmare and she going to wake up. "So you pretended to be employed with the forest service because, like everyone else over the last five years, you thought I played a major role in my husband's disappearance."

A white ring encircled his lips. She thought he might be ill, but it couldn't compare to the sickness pervading her soul.

"I approached your case like any other. Since you were still a person of interest to the police, I started with you first so I could learn for myself if you had a motive for wanting your husband dead or not."

"When did you start your investigation?"

"A week ago Friday. I've worked on it every spare moment."

Blaire could hardly take it in. "H-how did you dare take me around your son?" she stammered.

"After I told you about Josh's accident, your eyes spilled over and you asked if I had any pictures of him. That's when I learned one of the most important things about you."

Don't listen to him, Blaire.

"But you still don't know *the* most important thing because you don't have any proof." She took an unsteady breath. "Under the circumstances I suppose I should thank you for not taking things any further the other night. You could have," she admitted honestly, "and we both know I wouldn't have fought you."

"Your honesty is another thing I admire about you."

He had an answer for everything. "What's your real name?"

"Caige Dawson."

"Cage?" she mocked.

"With an *i*. It's an old English word meaning a man who builds cages."

"How apropos. I have to admit you're good at what you do. But I guess a crash course in oak wilt suppression was all part of a day's work for you." His abilities were extraordinary. Blaire could admit that. "You had me totally fooled," she said with deep bitterness.

"It was the only way for me to find out the truth about you."

She shook her head. "The truth. What's that? I don't understand why you didn't just wait until the end of the week and then leave like any temp would do. I would never have known I'd been conned all this time."

"Because I didn't want things to go any further between us until you knew the truth about *me*. I've done undercover work before, but your case has been different and we both know it."

Now what was he saying? She wanted to trust him, but this had come as such a shock, she was torn up inside.

"Whether you believe me or not, in my gut I know you had nothing to do with your husband's disappearance."

Tears stung her eyelids, but she absolutely refused to let them fall. "Your gut, huh?"

His chest rose and fell visibly. "It's never failed me yet. At this point, I need your cooperation. Only you can provide certain answers I couldn't get out of you while I was undercover."

She closed her eyes tightly. "What answers?" she cried. "I told the police everything I ever knew about anything. They must have reams of testimony from me."

"They do, and I've read through them all. But this is a new investigation on a cold case. I'll be asking questions no one else thought to ask. I'm on your side, Blaire."

How desperately she wanted to believe it. "If you were on my side, you wouldn't have kissed me," she bit out, avoiding his gaze. He had no idea how deep her feelings went. She hated it that everything had changed, that he wasn't the person she thought he was.

"I tried hard not to," he said in a husky voice. His nearness was too much.

"You didn't try hard enough. That was really taking unfair advantage."

"I know, but if you were a man and could have seen how beautiful you looked in the glow of the Christmas tree lights, you would understand."

She moaned inwardly. "I thought a Ranger was supposed to be beyond worldly temptations."

He was good. So good she was dissolving right in front of him.

A harsh laugh escaped his throat. "Only in the storybooks. My grandfather was a Ranger and he was one of the most human men I ever knew. If we're talking fantasies, I'm having one right now. It's the same one I had last week about cornering you up in a tree like this where we could really get into each other's arms."

The same fantasy had been in her mind for days now. "Stop it, Jack! I mean Caige."

"I answer to either name the way you say it," he replied in a seductive voice.

She couldn't take any more of this. "If you'll go down the tree, I'll follow."

"Only if you'll make me a promise."

He'd keep her up here until she gave in. "What is it?"

"That after we finish our work and go back to the office, I can come over to your town house."

"So you can look around?"

"That, and other things."

Her pulse raced. "After five years and two moves, I'm afraid there isn't anything to see."

"I'll be the judge of that. You still have your pictures of Nate."

She nodded. "They're stored in a box in the closet."

"If it'll be too painful for you, I could drop by there when you aren't home in order to spare you the grief."

Yes, it would be painful, but not for the reasons Caige was thinking. "The pictures will need explanations. Who else but me could give them to you?"

"Thank you for going along with me on this. I'll order us pizza."

"What about Josh? If you're not home on time, he's going to miss you."

"Elly will tend him. I've already made the arrangements."

So he'd already been planning this confession.

Blaire thought he was going to say something else, then thought the better of it. He moved down the tree with astonishing agility. She waited before taking her turn. This time there was no chance of her jumping on top of him by accident because he'd already started for the truck.

When she got closer, she saw him reach for something on the asphalt. Guilt brought heat to her cheeks when she realized it was his badge. But she wasn't going to apologize. He had to know how betrayed she felt.

She got in the cab with an aching heart. She was no longer out doing her work with Jack Lignell from the Trees for Texas program. The impossibly attractive male driving the Department of Forestry truck was none other than Captain Caige Dawson of the legendary Texas Rangers.

The man she loved now was heading a new investigation to find out what had happened to the man she'd loved five years ago. Things like this just didn't happen.

Chapter Seven

Caige followed Blaire's instructions to the Great Hills area of northwest Austin where she lived. A charming little brook with stands of hardwoods surrounded the cluster of Tudor-style town houses. Once he'd parked his car in one of the adjacent guest stalls, he reached for the manila envelope on the seat and headed for her condo, the third one on the left down the walkway.

He found the front door ajar and he could see a set of stairs going up from the small entrance hall. To the left was the living room. As he moved inside and shut the door, the first thing he noted with satisfaction was the poinsettia he'd given her. She'd put it on the light honey-stained wood-and-glass coffee table.

Flanking that were two comfortable-looking leather chairs in a caramel color. Matching stained end tables with glass inserts had been placed on either side of the couch upholstered in an off-white crewel-embroidered fabric. The fat brass-and-glass lamps made a stunning accompaniment. On the opposite side of the room sat her baby grand piano in a pecan-wood finish.

He didn't see any pictures of her husband. While he was admiring the large framed Renoir print of two girls at a piano on the wall, Blaire came down the stairs with a packing carton. She put it on the floor too fast for him to help her.

"You've created a beautiful home, Blaire." She was a woman of many surprising talents.

"Thank you. I'm sure you'd like to freshen up. The bathroom is around the corner, first door on the left."

He nodded. "On the way here, I phoned for pizza and salad."

"You didn't need to do that."

"I wanted to. I'll be right back."

The thing he'd feared had happened. Now that she knew the truth, she was already putting emotional barriers between them. When he rejoined her, she'd set the contents of the box on the chairs and couch to make it easier for him.

By the time the pizza arrived, he'd gone through the albums and loose photographs. He'd asked her to identify certain people, but nothing helped him. The pictures of her and Nate revealed what looked to be a blissfully happy couple. She'd worn her hair longer then. Though she'd been an exceptionally good-looking woman, he thought she was even more attractive now.

Her husband reminded him of the kind of preppy, well-groomed, well-dressed male who radiated success. In the photographs, he sported a nice tan. Farley would have carried off the golf-pro image without problem.

Blaire called to him from the kitchen—their pizza was waiting. He went back down the hall to the combined kitchen and dining room. She'd set the white dining-room table for them and had made coffee.

Before he sat down, he wandered around, taking in her herb garden and the two potted flowering lemon trees. Under the tube lights beneath the cupboard she'd placed a dozen pots of various violets. On another counter sat three baskets of pink azaleas.

"I like what you've done to your condo," he murmured before staring at her. "The yin is in the living room, the yang is in here."

"Evidence of my eclectic personality."

He had the feeling she was marking time, waiting for him to eat and leave. It was understandable considering the shock he'd given her today. After he'd eaten a few slices of pizza, he opened the envelope he'd brought and put an eight-by-ten glossy black-and-white photograph near her plate.

"Take a good look."

She stopped munching her salad long enough to study it. "That's the Dunn funeral. Oh, my heavens— Nate and I are in it!" she blurted. "Where did this come from?"

"The police files."

He saw her shudder.

"More often than not a detective will have pictures taken at the funeral of a murder victim in case the killer shows up. Do you see anyone you recognize? Examine it carefully. Whatever you tell me could be of vital importance."

"I went for Nate's sake," she said in an unsteady voice, "but they were all strangers to me."

"Did he introduce you to anyone?"

"No. We got there just before it started. That's why

we were in the background. The minute it was over we had to leave because I had a class and he had to get back to the bank."

"Can you remember if your husband spoke to anyone there?"

She rubbed her forehead. "I'm trying to think. The only thing I do recall was one older woman who broke down crying several times. It was heartbreaking. I assumed it was Mr. Dunn's mother."

"This woman here?" Caige pointed to a female figure in the photograph.

"Yes."

"Is the man holding her arm Mr. Dunn's brother? He's too young to be her husband."

"It couldn't be a brother. Nate said Mr. Dunn was an only child, like he was." Blaire flashed Caige an anxious glance. "Do you think it might be his caddy Ron holding on to her?"

"Maybe." He put the photo back in the envelope and finished eating his food. She'd lost interest in hers.

"The person who killed Mr. Dunn could have kidnapped my husband and killed him."

"Anything's possible." He put down his fork. "Blaire? The day you met Nate at the football game, was he sitting with friends?"

She looked surprised by his question. "He said he'd been with friends higher up in the bleachers. When he saw me, he decided to come down and talk to me."

Caige would have done the same thing. Blaire stood out wherever she went. "Did he have a best friend?"

"Sheldon Peterson, his friend from the bank. You saw him in the wedding album."

"I'm talking someone from the past. The reason I ask is because the pictures from that box don't show that he had any other close friends."

She frowned. "He told me *I* was his best friend. Before that he had to work too many jobs through high school and college to have much of a social life."

"What about Danny Dunn? Did you invite him to your wedding?"

"No."

"Didn't you think it odd considering Nate had spent so much time with him?"

"Yes. In fact, I said the same thing to Nate, but he insisted they weren't friends in that way. He wouldn't presume, so that was the end of it."

Caige was starting to dig deep, and he knew Blaire didn't like it. "I find it odd you still refer to him as Mr. Dunn. Why do you do that?"

Color seeped into her cheeks. "Because he was only Mr. Dunn to me. I never met him." She was holding back something.

"Didn't you want to meet him?"

"Of course."

"But your husband didn't want to introduce you. Don't hate me for this, but did it ever occur to you your husband could have had a gay side he didn't want you to know about?"

She got out of her seat and clung to the back of it. Her complexion had paled. "It never crossed my mind because our love life was satisfactory to me."

Caige studied her trembling figure. "Why didn't you ever go on those trips he took to San Diego?"

"Because we couldn't afford it."

"Yet he could afford expensive golf lessons."

"That was different. It was an investment for his career. We'd talked about it and planned it out. November would have been his last lesson if he hadn't disappeared."

"What about the money for rental cars, hotels and meals while he was on those trips?"

"Mr. Dunn had a place down there and arranged everything for Nate. He did it in exchange for Nate caddying for him when Ron wasn't available."

Blaire had a flaw, the same flaw plaguing millions of women who asked no questions of husbands who might be untrustworthy. "Did you always drive him to the airport and pick him up?"

"I took him the first time. After that, he just took his car and parked it in the short-term parking."

"How long was he gone for each time?"

"He left Friday night and came home Sunday morning."

After swallowing the last of his coffee, Caige got to his feet. "Didn't you start to question the setup even a little bit?"

Her eyes flashed an icy blue. "After a couple of months I hated it, but he always phoned me while he was gone, and because he always came home so happy and encouraged over the improvement in his game, I didn't make an issue of it. Tally Isom told him he would make pro ranking before long.

"But after Mr. Dunn was killed and the police questioned anyone who knew him, including Nate, that's when he told me about Ron being Mr. Dunn's lover. I asked him if he gave the police that information. He said no because he didn't have proof. It was only conjecture on his part."

"Your husband withheld what could have been vital evidence in an ongoing murder case."

"I know. You can imagine how the whole thing frightened me. Part of me wondered if Nate had brought it up as his way of trying to tell me the truth about his own orientation." Her breath staggered. "If he and Mr. Dunn had been lovers, it would explain why he didn't want me to see them together.

"When Nate disappeared before I'd worked up the nerve to confront him, I felt like the world's biggest fool for having stayed in denial months too long because of my own fears."

"That's why you didn't tell any of this to the police?"

"Yes. Five years ago I was traumatized by what happened. I'd only been married eight months and doubted everything I ever knew. It's taken me years to think rationally."

"Did you ever confide this to your parents?"

"To my whole family. They didn't believe it, but then they liked him so much. Mark was the most vocal. Though he and Nate weren't ones who had anything in common or would ever do anything together by choice, he said I was crazy to think Nate was gay. I asked him how he knew. He said, 'It's just not Nate.'"

Caige had a hunch Mark knew what he was talking

about. Caige had his own theory that Nate's interest in Dunn had more to do with money while he climbed that golden ladder to the top of the golf world.

Blaire looked so vulnerable standing there clutching the chair, Caige wanted to carry her upstairs. But he didn't want her accusing him of taking advantage. Besides, this wasn't the time. She needed space to come to grips with the new reality that her husband's case had been reopened. For now, Caige was neither her friend nor her enemy. At the moment she despised his undercover tactics, with good reason.

"I'll let myself out and see you in the morning."

"I don't mean to be rude, but why bother to show up for work, Caige? I don't need a partner, and Stan arranged for that temp job because you're on police business. Perry will be back on Monday."

He stared her down. "Did it ever occur to you that I like working with you? If I thought I couldn't see you tomorrow, *I* might have a tantrum."

SHE FELT THE SAME WAY.

Blaire watched him leave. Though she wanted to call him back she couldn't, not when she was so churned up inside.

As soon as she heard the front door close, she hurried upstairs to her bedroom where she'd left her purse. Where was Danny Dunn's place in San Diego? She needed to make a phone call to find out. She called 411.

"I'd like the number for the Torrey Pines golf course in San Diego, California, please."

The automated message from the golf course gave

her a full menu from which to choose. She pressed the digit for the golf shop. It was eight-thirty here. That meant six-thirty there.

"Golf shop."

"Hi. I'm anxious to talk to anyone there who might have worked in your shop five years ago. Would that be possible?"

"I've been here close to ten. How can I help?"

"Do you remember Danny Dunn, the pro golfer from Austin, Texas?"

"No, that name doesn't ring a bell. I'll transfer you over to the pro shop. They'll know more."

She waited until another voice came on the line. "Pro shop."

"I need some information about a pro golfer who used to play there five years ago named Danny Dunn from Austin, Texas."

"Sorry. The name's not familiar and we're closing right now. Call the business office in the morning. Maybe they can help you."

They probably couldn't if Mr. Dunn hadn't been that remarkable. Certainly the two employees she'd just talked to had no patience to try and help her.

After she'd hung up, she reached for the phone directory and looked up Dunn. There were over two hundred Dunns listed. She went through each one looking for the Hyde Park area code. *Nothing.* If Mrs. Dunn was still alive, she probably had a cell phone like Blaire, and no one knew the number except close family and friends.

She buried her face in her hands. It was appalling how little she'd known about Nate's life away from her.

Blaire didn't have a phone number to call, or a person who knew Nate and could answer her questions. He'd kept so much from her.

But you let him, Blaire.

Caige's question still raced around in her mind. *Didn't you start to question the setup even a little bit?*

He had to think she was the most pathetic creature alive. She was humiliated and furious with herself. A throwback to the nineteenth century when a wife knew nothing about her husband's business and didn't dare ask. How insane was that when this was the new millennium?

With her adrenaline surging, she cleaned up the kitchen and put the box of pictures away. After she'd typed up her notes on today's appointments, she phoned her parents. They had a quick conversation, then she got ready for bed.

Still needing a distraction, she turned on the TV to a movie, if only for the noise. At four in the morning she awakened to static. For the rest of the night she lay there going over everything in her mind. By the time she walked into the office four hours later, she knew what she had to do in order to hold her head up around Caige.

When he walked in, everyone bantered with him. They liked "Jack" a lot already. He'd become a favorite person in no time at all. It killed her that he wouldn't be working here after Friday. By the new year he wouldn't even be living in Austin.

While he was in the middle of a chat with the guys, she finished making out their schedule. "Let's get going, Jack. We've got an appointment out in Vista Royale."

It would be a half hour drive, which ought to give her plenty of time to have a certain discussion with him.

"Slave driver!" Marty called to her.

Blaire smiled. "That's me!" She put a copy of their schedule on Sheila's desk and headed outside for her truck. Caige caught up to her and they took off.

"Was Josh upset when you got home so late?"

"I don't know if he measures time the same way we do, but he seemed happy to see me. We played for an hour before I put him down. Your pull ball is still his favorite toy."

"That makes me happy."

She felt his gaze studying her profile. "About yesterday, Blaire. I know I knocked the foundations out from under you. If there'd been any other way under heaven, I wou—"

"I'm glad it happened," she cut in on him. It was the truth. "You woke me up from that awful state of nothingness I've been wallowing in all this time. I brought it on myself. I don't mean Nate's disappearance. I'm talking about everything leading up to it, especially my passive role as a wife."

"Some might call it trust and see it as prudent."

"No," Blaire retorted. "It's called cowardice. I stopped asking questions for fear of arousing Nate's anger." She sighed heavily. "It was wrong of me to pretend everything was fine when it wasn't."

"We all do that," he muttered. "I closed my ears to my wife's pleading for me to quit the Rangers. Our marriage got off track long before Josh's accident because of my selfishness."

"Do you look at your career choice as selfish?"

He made an odd sound in his throat. "It's not exactly the easiest thing on a marriage."

"Your grandfather did it and managed to have a family, too. How did his marriage fare?"

"From what I could tell they were very happy, but my grandmother was the kind of woman who went along with things and never complained even if she wanted to. For all I know, she hated his job."

"Whether she did or didn't, she knew he was doing the work that made him happy, so that's why she went along with it. An unhappy man worries a lot of wives whose husbands are near retirement age."

He chuckled. "So I understand."

"My mother fears my dad will go into a nosedive after he leaves pharmaceuticals for good. She's trying to talk him into buying a franchise for a chocolate outlet so they can run it together."

"Your mother sounds like a very wise woman."

"She's always been forward-thinking. Not like someone you know who's sitting next to you."

"You're being too hard on yourself, Blaire."

"No more so than you beating yourself up on your career choice." She glanced at him. "Obviously you wanted to be a Ranger badly enough to leave Naylor. What's the reason you're planning to move back there after Christmas?"

"Josh is getting older and needs more attention outside of school. I can't provide it if I'm off on a case. With family close by, he'll get the added stimulation on a regular basis."

"Tell me something honestly. Would your wife have liked it if you'd gone back to ranching and moved there sooner?"

Caige shook his dark head without hesitation. "She's a big-city girl. The slow small-town life in Naylor was anathema to her. It would never have worked. I'm afraid Josh's brain injury was the final blow in a long line of hurts."

"You don't talk about her family. Did she have siblings?"

"No."

So Liz was an only child. Like Nate... Did that mean anything? Blaire scoffed at herself. Not really. She had two siblings and look at her!

While Caige was being exceptionally quiet, she saw a convenience store and pulled into the parking area in order to buy ice and treats. She offered to do the honors. When she returned with a sack of goodies and they were on the road again, she handed him a Milky Way bar. He was addicted to them. The way he tore off the paper and started munching, she figured it had brightened his spirits.

"Do you know, I lay awake for hours last night turning everything over in my mind? Around five this morning I came up with an idea."

"Go on." He reached in the sack for the diet cola, his other addiction. He sounded happier than before.

"I know it's five years after Nate's disappearance, but instead of crying about it, I want to become proactive because I'm sick and tired of the status quo. My parents are, too, or they wouldn't have approached Agent

Robbins again. As you said yesterday, we don't know if Nate is alive or dead. Therefore I've got a proposition for you."

He flashed her a half grin so beguiling, she could hardly breathe. "I love it already." Caige wasn't taking her seriously. Now it was her turn to drop her little bomb.

"Will you let me work with you to solve my case?"

"In what way?"

"In *every* way. It's why you went undercover. Now that you've told me the truth about yourself, you can fire all the questions you want at me and *I* can play an active part. You're the one with the law on your side, but I have ideas. Let me tell you what I did after you left last evening." In a few minutes she explained about her phone call to Torrey Pines.

That seemed to surprise him. He finished off his drink and put the can back in the bag. "It's nearly impossible getting answers out of people unless the police force them to talk."

"I found that out, but the fact remains someone has to know if Danny Dunn actually had a place there. I've come to the conclusion that Nate told me a lot of lies throughout our marriage and before. According to him, he had no living relatives. It's hard to know that much about a person when all you have is his word to go on."

"I'm sorry, Blaire." He sounded pained for her.

"Don't be. It's life. Looking back now, I find myself suspecting everything. So many little things I dismissed at the time are starting to make sense."

"Like what?"

"Like the Saturday I called the Hilly Heights golf shop to find out if Nate had come off the course with Mr. Dunn yet. We'd planned to go to lunch and do some shopping. But the answer I got was that Mr. Dunn hadn't been on the course, so my husband was probably out caddying for someone else. But that couldn't have been, or someone would have written it down.

"When I asked Nate about it, he told me Mr. Dunn had decided to take them to the newer Falconhead golf course where he liked to play. Apparently their game went on longer than they'd planned. My husband was always penitent and had an answer that made sense at the time."

Caige reflected for a minute. "I noticed you set up our first appointment at an address near the Bee Caves. It's not that far from Falconhead. Something tells me that wasn't a coincidence."

She gave him an impish smile. "No. I thought that after we finished our job, we could drive over there and ask some questions. I'm curious to find out how many times Mr. Dunn played there and who the caddy was. It should be in their records."

He flashed her a look that said he was impressed. It gave her the courage to tell him the rest.

"After the fiasco phone call to Torrey Pines, I tried to phone Danny Dunn's mother, but couldn't find the number. Yet after giving it serious thought, I decided she'd be the last person to know anything about the dark part of her son's life he chose to keep secret."

Caige's startled gaze swept over her as if he were

seeing her for the first time. "You really did have an epiphany last night."

She nodded. "After those men at Torrey Pines refused to give me the time of day, I thought long and hard about it. If you were really free to give this your all, 24/7, I believe in my heart you'd find out what happened to Nate much sooner than we think."

"Your faith in me is gratifying, but you have no proof of that," he said in a gravelly voice. For once she felt she'd caught him off guard. To hear this tough man sound so vulnerable caught at her emotions.

"To quote a certain Texas Ranger whose badge I threw at him yesterday during my tantrum, it's a feeling in my gut. The funny thing is, my gut instinct has never been wrong, either, especially about Nate. To my dismay, my huge character flaw was not *acting* on it, but those days are over."

"Will the real Blaire Koslov please stand up?"

She broke into laughter as he reached in the sack for a second Milky Way. He always ate two. "Your training as a pathologist would give you a definite edge if you ever wanted to go into law enforcement."

"No, no. I gladly leave that to an expert's expert like you. But I know I'll be much happier to tag along supplying moral support, snacks. Think of it this way. I'll be providing another mind for brainstorming. But not just anyone's mind!"

There was something else she could provide, too, but he wasn't ready to hear it yet. She knew he wasn't because he hadn't responded to her last remarks.

"Oh, dear," she said as they drew up to their first appointment. The telltale signs of disease made the trees stand out a mile.

"Oak wilt," Caige supplied. "It's everywhere. I see it in my sleep."

"Tell me about it."

They made quick work of taking samples and got back in the truck. Blaire was excited about reaching the golf course at Falconhead.

Maybe there was something wrong with her that she couldn't wait to find out if she was right and Nate had lied to her about even the little things like this. But they weren't little things if they all added up to a whole life based on lies. Somewhere along the way in her marriage, her love for him had slowly taken a downward turn, but she'd been too in denial to acknowledge it.

After they entered the Falconhead club, Blaire drew a lot of satisfaction watching Ranger Dawson in action. The respect the staff gave him for his authority, as well as the aura of the intimidating man himself, made it fascinating for her to watch. He had some photos of Nate he flashed from his wallet.

"I don't recognize him." To the manager's credit, he had all the employees hustling to provide answers. The guy in the golf shop couldn't have been more cooperative, but after looking through the records, he shook his head.

"Danny Dunn didn't play here often. When he did, he brought his own caddy, Ron Seeward." Blaire and Caige exchanged a private glance. "Word got around that he preferred the Bermuda-grass greens at Lost Pines. Maybe your husband caddied for him there."

"Maybe," Blaire murmured. "When I first met Nate, he did mention playing at Lost Pines, but he said *playing,* not *caddying.*" She supplied her own picture of Nate. "So none of you ever saw this man with Mr. Dunn? You're absolutely positive?"

Three of the men, seasoned golfers who would know, crowded around. "Sorry," they murmured. "We hope you find out what happened to him."

"So do I."

"Thank you for your help, gentlemen." Caige shot her a glance. "Shall we go?"

"Lie number one verified," she murmured once they were back at the truck. "Nate never went to Falconhead. Let's hurry and get our work done. I want to drive to Lost Pines."

"I think you've done enough police work for one day." He broke into a smile as he said it, but she didn't buy it.

"After working with you for a week, I can read you pretty well. What are you afraid of? That I might catch Nate in another lie and won't like it?"

Behind his silky black lashes, those silvery-gray eyes darkened with emotion.

She swallowed hard. "How many lies do you already know about?" Silence followed her question. "Caige?" she pressed him.

"Only one other verified lie so far."

"I see." Damn if her voice didn't tremble. "Well, it must be a whopper."

Chapter Eight

It was the whopper of whoppers.

Smothering a groan, Caige pulled out his cell phone to check his voice mail. Ernie. He played the message.

"We got a call from Mel's Public Shooting Range outside Burnet." That was sixty miles northwest of Austin. "The guy who runs it showed the flyer to his father, Mel, who's the owner. He recognized the photograph on the flyer—not the drawing—from a long time ago because of the bombshell brunette with him.

"They came several times in a black BMW convertible in their flashy clothes. He thought they might be film stars because he was good-looking and had that kind of tan you don't get in the States. But he said the name's wrong on the flyer. She called him Rick. He couldn't remember the last name and they don't keep records. Said he was a good shot and paid cash both times. This one's worth investigating."

Amen.

Caige had a dozen questions. Did Mel remember the make of gun? Did he see the license plate? How young was the woman? He needed a full description. Did she have pierced ears? Did she speak with an accent? Did they mention where they'd been or where they were going? Did either of them wear rings on their ring fingers?

"Caige?"

He put his phone back in his pocket and eyed Blaire. "Do you trust me?"

"What a question!" she cried. "You *know* I do."

"Then I'd rather not discuss all the aspects of your case until I've gathered some more facts."

"Without *me,* you mean."

"I didn't say that. I'm curious to see what we can find out at Lost Pines."

Farley's case seemed to be taking off in a new direction that might not have that much to do with Danny Dunn after all. But it wouldn't hurt to run by the other golf course in case Nate had been seen there using another name.

He picked up their schedule. "Let's figure out how we want to proceed so we end up there last."

"I already did." She started up the truck and turned on the radio. "Do you have a preference? Sports? Politics? Music?"

"Why don't you surprise me?" The air was thick with tension. She was trying so hard to be brave and positive about this. His respect for her was off the charts.

The scanner went from station to station until she left it on a classical-music station. Whoever was playing was a fabulous pianist. "Do you know this piece?"

"Yes. It's Grieg's 'First Piano Concerto.' Van Cliburn."

"It takes an artist to know one."

"There've been so many renditions of it over the years, you learn the ones you love."

"Do you love this one?"

"Yes," she whispered. "There are certain passages that ring out with emotion. You hear how this is surging?" He nodded. "He has the pacing right. Some artists play it too fast or too slow."

He sucked in his breath. "Have you played this concerto yourself?"

"Once upon a time. Naturally without a symphony," she added with a chuckle.

Blaire was that good? "Who's another one of your favorite composers?"

She gave him a little smile. "Have you got an hour?"

"When I was a police officer, one of my partners loved classical music. He had a preference for Bach and Handel."

"Did you like them?"

"To a degree, but I much prefer this. It grabs you by the throat."

Blaire chuckled. He hadn't expected her mood to lighten. It came as a relief because they had the rest of the day to get through. "When it grabs you by the heart, then you're truly hooked."

"I agree this is a beautiful piece. I presume you love Tchaikovsky, too. How would you like to go to the *Nutcracker* with me?"

"I haven't been in—" She stopped. "I'd love to."

"Good. I'll get tickets. I'm sorry to say it's one of the things Josh will never enjoy."

"There's always the next life."

He flicked her another glance. "That's what my father says when I get in one of my morose moods."

Her hands tightened on the steering wheel. "I'm finding out this life is shorter than I thought and time is fleeting. It wouldn't make sense to only be here for a little while and not have it go on in some new wonderful way."

Time *was* fleeting. Caige wanted to wrap up this case today and grab at his happiness, who happened to be sitting next to him.

After their next appointment, they stopped for Mexican food. Once back on the job, they finished out the day in record time. Before long they drove into Bastrop State Park and reached Lost Pines, one of four golf courses within the park's boundaries.

While Caige let Blaire ask the questions, he passed around the photos of Nate. No one recognized him, but they remembered Danny Dunn. "Oh, yeah. He and Ron used to hang out here with some of the guys, betting on the horses over in Manor. It's closed down now."

Manor, once known as Casino City. Caige wasn't the least bit surprised by this piece of information. Dirty money had kept Danny Dunn afloat. Did it fund Nate, too, or did his money come from another source? Caige was getting closer, but he couldn't make it happen fast enough to suit him.

On their way back to Austin, Blaire said, "Did your housekeeper get special training to learn how to take care of Josh?"

His breath caught. She'd surprised him again with the direction of her question. "No. I taught her everything."

"Do you think you could teach me? I mean, if you trusted me enough?"

The blood hammered in his ears. "What are you getting at?"

"While we were at Lost Pines, I was given a little glimpse of what you do to try to get even one tiny piece of information out of people. As I see it, you need a lot of time and freedom to work a case like mine. It must drive you crazy to learn something, but not be able to act on it right away because of other commitments."

"That's true."

"Now that I know you're a Ranger, it's driving me crazy, too. I want you to solve this case as fast as you can because it's my life hanging in the balance here. So I was thinking of giving up my forest-service job in order to come work full-time for you."

What? He had to be hearing things.

"It would only be until Nate's body is found. After hearing about Danny Dunn's interest in gambling, I'm pretty sure Nate was involved, too, and was killed by the same people who killed Danny. You're onto a good lead, Caige. With Elly leaving, I can help by taking care of Josh so you don't have to look for another house-keeper."

Tight bands constricted his breathing. To think of Blaire sleeping under his roof... "You have no idea what's involved."

"Did Elly?"

His head reared. "She's an older widow who has raised a family. You're—"

"I'm a nothing at the moment," she cut in, "but I want to be a something."

The pathos in those words moved him unbearably.

"I'll be honest. My life has been empty in that one area where I need to be needed. When I was at your house the other night playing with Josh, it felt good, you know?"

"He's not easy, Blaire. There are times when it's damn frustrating."

Her fathomless blue eyes beseeched him. "Is anything easy that's really worthwhile? I like children and have taught music lessons to a lot of them. It would be a privilege to take care of him. He's adorable, and you're on the brink of making a big move to Naylor with no help when Elly's gone."

"This case might not get solved for a long time." There was no way on earth he'd be able to keep his hands off her. The whole idea was impossible.

"It doesn't matter to me. I can't declare Nate legally dead for two more years anyway. Now that you're working on it, nothing's more important to me than knowing what happened to Nate so I can be free to get on with my life. With the office closing down for the holidays starting next week, Stan will have plenty of time to find a replacement."

"Blaire—"

"Whether you believe me or not," she went on, "when you told me you'd be losing Elly, I was considering asking for the job as her replacement before you told me you weren't Jack Lignell."

Don't listen to her, Dawson. The silken chains were tightening around him faster than he could fight them.

"I can always go back to the forest service, but I have to tell you, Josh really got to me. To care for him is something I want to do while you put your life on the line for me. I'm not unaware that there's danger involved. Danny Dunn's death and my husband's disappearance are a case in point."

"That goes with the job, Blaire, but you don't know what you'd be getting into."

"You don't think I could be the right kind of caretaker for Josh. Is that it? Or a decent housekeeper? I'm a pretty good cook. Ask my family."

He gritted his teeth in exasperation. She had it all wrong. "I didn't say any of those things." If she had any idea what was going on inside him…

"I know. That's what is making me nervous, because I'm afraid you're thinking them."

"You don't know what in the hell I'm thinking." He was terrified by the thrill of excitement that shot through his body when he even entertained the thought.

"Oh, yes, I do. You're worried about what your family might say, or your colleagues. Most likely you're nervous I'm trying to proposition you in the good old-fashioned sense of the word and you don't want me getting any ideas about it being a permanent arrangement."

He was nervous, all right, but only because if he hired her, he'd wouldn't be able to let her go when the time came, even if she wanted to leave. Caige knew himself too well.

"But that isn't my motive and deep down you have to know it!"

He did know it. Her motive was pure. His wouldn't be so pure if he gave in.

"Our situation is unique. This would be a business transaction like you have with Elly. Nothing more, nothing less. You have to find someone else to replace her right away. Why not me?"

Caige fought to suppress a moan of half joy, half despair.

"I'm the one person who will understand your long absences and strange hours and never complain. How could I when you'll be doing all of it for *me?*"

They'd arrived back at the office. She drove him to his car to let him out. "Will you at least think about it?" she asked without looking at him.

Talk about teetering on the edge...

"I'll sleep on it." What a joke that was. There'd be no sleep for him tonight.

"Thank you for not saying no to me outright. For the first time in years, I feel there's hope for life to be good again," she said in a hushed tone.

BLAIRE SENT OFF THE SAMPLES before driving straight to her parents' home. They lived only a mile from her condo. Her pretty, dark blonde mother was in the kitchen fixing dinner. "Mom?"

"Darling!" Mrs. Koslov stopped what she was doing to hug her daughter. "Why didn't you let me know you were coming?"

"I didn't know. I just found myself driving here. I need to talk to you."

"Of course. Your dad won't be home for a while. Sit down." But Blaire remained standing. "What's wrong?" She cupped her daughter's face. "What's happened?"

"I hardly know where to start."

"The beginning will do."

"Oh, Mom—I think I've done a terrible thing, and now I don't know how to undo it."

Her mother blinked before her hands fell away from Blaire's cheeks. "What's this supposedly terrible thing?"

"Today I applied for the job of caretaker to a brain-injured boy. I practically begged his father. Now I'm afraid I've put him in an impossible position."

Her mother sat down in the nearest chair. "Who is this man?"

Blaire hugged her arms to her waist. "He's a captain in the Texas Rangers. After you and Dad talked to Agent Robbins, he assigned Caige Dawson to my case."

"That happened faster than I would have thought. When did you meet him?"

"I-It's a long story." Her voice faltered. She sank down on the other chair, and suddenly it all came pouring out. Blaire didn't stop until she'd told her mother everything about the investigation, about Jack Lignell before he turned into Caige, about his little boy.

Her mother was silent for a long time. Her eyes searched Blaire's. "Are you in love with this man?"

"Yes," she said with an ache in her voice.

"That sounded definite." She cocked her head. "Is he in love with you?"

"I don't know. Sometimes when he looks at me, I can hardly breathe, but it's very complicated. He's the most fabulous man I ever met in my life. You should see the way he loves his son. It brings tears to your eyes."

Her mom sat back in the chair. "I take it he hasn't hired you yet."

"No. He said he'd sleep on it. I don't think he wants to hire me, but if I call him and tell him I've changed my mind, he'll wonder what kind of woman he's dealing with."

"If his mind is already made up against hiring you, does it matter what he thinks?"

"You *know* it matters to me, but if it will relieve his mind of a burden, then I ought to phone him right now."

"Did you make the offer in order to get closer to him?"

Blaire jumped up from the chair. "I don't think so. If you'd met him, you would know he's the person who can find out what happened to Nate, but with his house-keeper leaving, he'll have to find another woman and train her. It'll take time away from his work. If I take care of Josh, he'll have that time much sooner."

"He was right when he said it wouldn't be easy."

"I'm sure it won't be, but being in hell for five years hasn't been easy, either."

The next thing she knew, her mom's arms went around her. "I think it was the most *un*-Blaire-ish thing my cautious daughter has ever done in her life. If you want my opinion, I'm all for it."

"You mean it?" she cried. Her mother nodded. "That means more to me than you know." She wiped her eyes. "Thanks for talking to me. I've got to go, but I'll keep you posted."

Blaire returned to her town house in a better frame of mind than when she'd driven to her parents' house. Her mom had given her that shot of confidence she needed. Still feeling jumpy after making that extraordinary proposal to Caige, she decided a shower and shampoo might help her to relax.

After leaving the bathroom, she put on a long-sleeved navy sweat suit and was ready to go downstairs to make herself a sandwich when she heard her doorbell ring. Maybe her dad had gotten home from work and they'd decided to come over to talk some more.

She left her room in bare feet and hurried downstairs to get the door. "Mom?" she said before unlocking it.

"No. It's Caige."

He'd come over without calling? That had to be a bad sign. Her body broke out in a cold sweat.

"Hi," he said when she found the nerve to open the door. Her tall, ruggedly handsome Ranger had showered and changed into jeans and a blue T-shirt. He held a carryall bag in one hand. Josh, who was dressed in the same kind of outfit, had hold of his other hand and clung to him.

Caige's slate-gray eyes traveled over her face and figure, missing nothing, from her bare toes to the crown of her still slightly damp hair. He'd caught her without makeup, not that she wore much more than lipstick.

"We were out for our evening ride and wondered

if you were up for some company. That is, if you're free. I'm curious to see how he responds to you in an unfamiliar environment."

This was a test. He was giving her a chance. *Don't blow it, Blaire. Don't frighten Josh by being too friendly.*

She lowered her head to his son's eye level. "How are you, Josh? Do you want to come in?" Blaire stood aside so they could enter. She noticed the boy took little steps, as if he were hesitant, but, to her relief, he didn't try to pull back from his father as he shut the door.

Without saying anything to Caige, she reached for the bag. "What do we have in here?" She sat in the middle of the floor and pulled out some toys. The pull ball was something she knew how to set up, so she put it in front of her and started playing with it.

Josh let go of his father's hand and sat down by her. He pulled on it and watched it move with the same intensity as before. Pleased to see his concentration, she slowly got up and moved over to the piano bench.

He didn't seem to notice until she played a scale at a quiet pitch so it wouldn't startle him. His dark head turned in her direction. He sat there looking up at her with those clear blue eyes. She played it again and held her breath. Suddenly that sweet smile broke out on his face and he walked over to her.

"Do you want to play?" She took hold of his left hand and placed it on the keys.

He pulled away from her with strength that shouldn't have surprised her. He didn't want her touching him. First big mistake, but she didn't react, just sat there. Her patience won out when a half minute later he pounded the keys with the flat of both hands. He liked doing that.

She lifted her head to discover Caige's attentive gaze on her. He was smiling, not only with his mouth but with his eyes. Blaire felt as if the clouds had opened up to let the sun shine through, filling those dark places that hadn't known light for years.

Instinct told her to move so his father could join in. While she turned off the music from the pull ball, Caige came around to sit and pulled Josh onto his lap. Together they made a cacophony of sounds. After a minute Josh stopped playing and turned his head to kiss his father half a dozen times. Every time he did that, Blaire wanted to break down in tears because the little boy was so loving.

Except that Josh really wasn't a little boy. He was eight years old, tall and well-built for his age. Soon he'd be moving into adolescence. If Blaire were to have the responsibility of him when Caige wasn't home, she needed to learn a lot in a short period of time.

With the two of them preoccupied, she hurried in the kitchen and brought out an opened box of crackers. If he could eat pancakes, she figured crackers were all right. She undid the wrapping on a new pack, then sat back down on the floor and started examining the other toys.

There was a mini popper and a domelike game called a twinkler. Both were activated by a switch. When she pressed on the mini popper, it played music while things popped. It caught Josh's attention.

He wiggled from his father's arms and came over to

sit down by her. She purposely reached for a cracker and ate it. He reached for one, too. Pretty soon Caige joined them on the floor and they all played with a toy. Every once in a while Josh smiled at his daddy. After eating another cracker, he smiled at her. A true smile. It made her giddy with happiness.

While Caige's head was bent over the twinkler he said, "Why don't you play something for us? A little tune."

Without drawing attention to herself, she eased up from the floor and went over to the piano. She started playing the first piece she'd ever learned from her piano teacher. She sang it as she played. "Here we go, up a row, to a birthday party. Dolly dear, sandman's here. Soon you will be sleeping." Good old John Thompson technique.

Surprisingly, Josh got up and walked over. He started playing again. To make room for him, she moved her hands two octaves lower. She played and sang the same words again and again while he pounded. He just smiled and smiled as if they were doing the most fabulous duet in the world together.

Caige had come over and was lounging against the harp of the piano. She caught his glance. His luminescent gray eyes had glazed over with emotion. There were moments of joy in life, and this was one of them.

Josh never tired. She decided to change the music and started playing a tune from the film version of *Snow White*. He stopped long enough to look at her. Blaire started singing the words and got animated. "Hi ho, hi ho, it's off to work we go. Tra la la la la, tra la la la la lo, hi ho, hi ho."

He started playing again, but this time he pounded harder and louder. Even before Caige came around to pull him off the bench, she realized she'd put too much into it and had overstimulated him.

"I'm sorry," she whispered, anxious to put things right. They'd been getting along so beautifully.

His dark brows knitted together. "What are you talking about?" He walked Josh back over to the toys.

"I overexcited him."

"There's nothing wrong with that. I was afraid he was going to ruin your piano. He doesn't know boundaries. Your beautiful instrument is simply another toy to him."

Relief swept through her. "I was afraid I'd done something wrong."

He shook his head. "Every instinct of yours has been right on. He's had a wonderful time tonight and doesn't know when to quit."

She smiled. "I noticed."

"I need to get him to bed. Thank you for letting us drop in on you unannounced."

"I loved it." Blaire wanted to ask them to stay, but this wasn't the time. She helped put the toys in the bag and gave Josh another cracker. The two of them walked to the front door. She followed.

Caige darted her a level glance she couldn't read. "See you in the morning."

The morning. She would lie awake all night wondering if he was going to let her train for the job or not.

"Good night, Josh." The boy just kept on walking while he clung to his father's hand.

How much he computed was impossible to guess, but she had an idea it was a lot more than could be observed with the naked eye. Music had found its way into his little psyche and he'd liked it. Unless Caige told her differently, she would treat his son like any boy, yet follow his guidelines.

Blaire watched them walk along the pathway until she couldn't see them anymore. When she shut and locked the door, she was so wound up with excess energy, she did something for herself she hadn't done in years; she sat down at the piano.

Without conscious thought she began playing "The Little Shepherd" from Debussy's *Children's Corner*. The plaintive motif suited her mood, reminding her of Josh, who was like a sweet lamb needing shepherding.

It all started coming back. Mistakes didn't matter. Too many years of practice had inscribed the music in her head. Soon she was going through a whole repertoire of pieces she used to teach her students.

Because of Josh, a window had opened, letting in a long-forgotten breeze. Before long, she was playing everything from Brahms to Beethoven. Her thoughts were on the concerto she and Caige had listened to in the truck.

She turned to Grieg and played his "Wedding Day at Troldhaugen." The music had been locked in her heart for too long. After playing the last notes, she discovered tears of release streaming down her face. They'd been falling a long time because her top was soaked.

To her shock it was after midnight. Recognizing she'd turned a corner in her life, she turned out the lights and went up to bed, eager for the day to come. She'd be seeing Caige again.

AFTER PUTTING JOSH TO BED, Caige went into his den and got online to order tickets for the *Nutcracker* for Friday night. Blaire's fabulous musical talent was obvious and he was looking forward to going to the ballet with her. But something else had happened tonight that put him in awe of her. It was the way she'd handled Josh with such amazing sensitivity.

As he'd watched the two of them at the piano, he could tell they were both loving it in their own ways, as if they were kindred spirits relating on a level known only to them. It was a magical moment, one he'd never forget.

Once he'd sent off emails to Mac and Ernie updating them on today's events, he got ready for bed, but sleep didn't come for a while.

Until he'd gone to her town house tonight, he didn't honestly know what he would tell her in the morning. But as the evening had progressed, an idea had come to him he felt could work. While they were up in the trees the next day taking samples, he broached the subject with her.

"Did you have plans for Friday night?" he called to her.

"No," she answered back from the tree next to him. The two trees didn't look like they had the same problem, but something was wrong with both of them.

"That's good because I got us tickets for the ballet."

"Oh, thank you! I can't wait to see it!"

"I'm excited, too. It's been a long time for me."

She hadn't done a lot of talking since they'd left the office. He knew she was waiting for him to say something about Josh. He put the sample in the bag and jumped to the ground. After slipping it in the ice chest, he walked over to the base of her tree and looked up.

"I had a talk with Elly this morning."

Blaire's hands stilled on the branch, letting him know he had her full attention.

"Christmas is only nine days away. She's leaving for her sister's on Monday. That gives us the rest of this week for you to be her shadow."

"Oh, Caige—you're sure?" The excitement in her voice lit him up like a firecracker. She scrambled down to the joint in the tree. Her eyes looked like hot blue stars. After she dropped to the ground with her saw and sample, it took all his willpower not to pick her up and crush her in his arms.

"As sure as I can be about anything." He put her things away, having needed something to do with his hands so he wouldn't grab her. "I put in a call to Stan and explained what was going on with us. He's willing to let today be your last day so you'll have the rest of the week to observe Elly's routine with Josh. We're supposed to go into the office after lunch and he'll talk to us." He picked up the ice chest and they started walking toward the truck.

She followed behind him. "Did he seem upset?"

"No. He knows we're trying to solve your case. I told

him we were a team." That was the way Caige had to look at it if this was going to work.

"Stan's a good man."

Caige was driving today. On the way to their next appointment he told her what was on his mind. "I'd like to try an experiment with Josh that means you wouldn't have to give up your town house."

A puzzled look entered her eyes.

"If he spent some time at your place this week and got used to it, then you and I could go back and forth as necessary without his world falling apart. I believe the piano was a bigger hit with him than you realize. I'd love him to be more exposed to it."

"You mean you'd let him sleep over with me sometimes?"

"Only if I had to be out of town and it was necessary. Sometimes you'll be taking him to school and picking him up. It might be convenient for you to sleep at your house when you wanted, or sleep at mine. We could store a few toys at both places. Elly didn't have a home, but you do. It would allow you to keep your life intact, yet expand the walls of Josh's world."

And maybe Caige would be able to handle their close association without breaking all the rules.

"It's a wonderful idea, but only if Josh is comfortable with it. Please don't worry. I can always rent my town house."

"Let's hope it doesn't have to come to that." Caige had other plans in mind for the future. "One of the things I'm hoping you can do is get him to ride on the bus again. Something upset him and he hasn't wanted to ride it ever since."

"Would it help if I went on the bus with him? I could stay at his school and then ride it home with him."

"We'll talk to his teacher about it. After this week he won't be going to school again until after New Year's, so it's a ways away yet. In fact, it's all tentative, depending on how you feel after spending the rest of the week with him."

"I already know how I'll feel. It's Josh who has to get used to me." She made a betraying motion with her hands. "What if he doesn't, Caige?"

He wasn't immune to the anxiety in her voice. "It was iffy with Elly and the two other housekeepers before her, but eventually things worked out. I can tell you one thing. He loved the music last night. That's something none of the others could give him. You got to him in a way no one has before."

"Don't they have music at his school?" Her earnestness reached out to him.

He pulled up to the house where they had their next appointment and turned off the motor. "Some." Caige turned to look at her. She was such a raving beauty, he ached to touch that face and kiss her for a long, long time.

"But there's only one Blaire Koslov. Terrific as Mrs. Wright is, she doesn't look like you, talk like you, play like you or have your personality. When you started singing 'Hi Ho' in a voice that sounded exactly like one of those endearing dwarves, my son's eyes danced. He was enchanted.

"And so was I," Caige drawled. "I'd like the enchantment to go on and on. It's clear to me Josh has already accepted you on some level. Things are going to work out. I know something else, too." His voice hardened. "I'm going to find out what happened to your husband. I swear it."

Blaire took a deep breath and reached for his hand, clinging to it with all her might. He looked down. No gesture had ever had the power to move him the way that did.

Chapter Nine

On Friday morning Caige went into headquarters for a strategy meeting with Mac and Ernie. They'd planned to meet in Mac's office. When Caige walked in and saw the coffee and doughnuts, it surprised him. Normally his boss didn't provide goodies unless there was a special reason. Caige poured himself some brew while he waited.

His two mentors were like family, always ready to help, always prepared to lay down their lives for a brother if necessary. Because of Blaire, both men knew this case was different from all the others. They saw right through him, but, like the good men they were, they kept the comments down and concentrated on the business at hand.

The situation at home had altered so drastically, Caige felt as he had when he was a young rookie on the Austin Police Force. Back then he'd leave for work without a worry to distract him from the task at hand. Blaire was the reason for the euphoria infecting him. They'd known each other only two weeks, yet he couldn't seem to remember his life without her now.

Already there were changes. She'd driven with him

to take Josh to school all three mornings. His son smiled at her more and more. Little by little they were making progress. Knowing Blaire was there to take over made Elly happier, too. As far as Caige could tell, the women got along as if they'd known each other for ages. Josh was the common thread bonding the two of them.

Tonight Caige would be taking Blaire to the ballet. He was counting the hours. Elly had agreed to babysit one last time. Caige dared to believe his life had entered a shining new era that could become his reality. All he had to do was find Nate Farley, dead or alive.

Mac finally came into the office, followed by Ernie, who shut the door. Caige had been waiting long enough to have eaten a second doughnut. They looked at him with that secret kind of smile that meant something was up.

"What?"

Mac patted him on the shoulder. "Once again you're the man of the hour." Both men sat down.

"I don't have a clue what you're talking about."

"The book's been officially closed on the Danny Dunn murder case."

"Without you, it might never have been solved," Ernie declared. "Congratulations. Word has it you'll be receiving another commendation from the governor. That makes quite a few so far."

Caige put the mug down so hard, he spilled his coffee. "You're conning me, right?" He reached for a napkin to clean up the mess.

"You want chapter and verse, I guess." Mac grinned. "Using your tips that we passed on to the police investigating the case, it turns out Farley was right. Dunn had a lover, but his name was Charlie Beck. Dunn was at Ron Seeward's house the night Charlie showed up with a gun, accusing him of having an affair with Ron.

"There was a fight and several shots were fired, one killing Dunn. Since the three of them had been living on illegal gambling winnings from the racetrack in Manor, Ron didn't want to be involved in any of it. He looked the other way when Charlie dumped the body on the golf course."

This kind of news blew Caige's mind.

"The police entered Charlie Beck's apartment with a warrant and found the gun. The ballistics matched. Beck broke down and ratted on Ron Seeward. The police got a warrant to search Seeward's place and found evidence that it had been the crime scene.

"Beck was arrested for murder. Seeward's been arrested for impeding a criminal investigation, tampering with a crime scene and withholding evidence. The list goes on. Both men were charged with racketeering. The police have a full confession from them that will bring more arrests."

Mac leaned forward, munching on his second doughnut. "It was *you* who attacked the Farley case and was running down leads in the first two hours. The news that you cracked the Dunn murder will be plastered all over the media by morning. That's great work, my boy."

The news should have been gratifying to Caige, but his good mood had vanished. "Except that the wrong case has been wrapped up," he bit out. "There's still nothing leading me directly to Farley. I want the chance to interrogate both men. They know plenty they're not telling."

"Why don't you do that as soon as our meeting is over? Right now let's see what you've come up with so far. What about the tip from that Mel at the shooting gallery in Burnet?"

"I've thought about it. He identified Farley from the photo, but Farley was with a brunette driving a BMW, and he was using the name Rick. I'm not sure we can count on testimony like that when it was more than five years ago. I'm not ruling it out, but it's not proof."

"What else?"

"Bits and pieces I still can't tie together. The manager of the Sterling Luxury Condos was supposed to be available on Wednesday, but when I called, his voice mail was still on. We know Farley paid cash to send flowers to a woman named Janie Pettigrew in La Jolla. We have proof he flew to San Diego every fourth weekend for the months he was married to Blaire. We have evidence he didn't take lessons at Torrey Pines from Tally Isom. All roads seem to lead to California."

Ernie poured himself more coffee. "I'm still phoning every Janie Pettigrew listed in San Diego County."

Mac's brows lifted. "Did you ask Blaire if she's ever heard of a Janie Pettigrew?"

Caige heaved a troubled sigh. "Not yet. I'd hoped that if there was a woman involved, I'd have all my ducks lined up first." His elbows rested on the table while he pressed his laced fingers against his forehead. "If there's no other way, then I'll have to ask her."

Both men nodded.

"Go on over to the jail," Mac told him. "See what you can pull out of Seeward. You're getting closer, Caige. It won't be long. I can smell success around the corner."

He wanted to believe it. His life depended on it. "Thanks for the grub and the talk." Caige pushed himself away from the table, anxious to confront the caddy who, he knew in his gut, could provide more answers. Caige needed to give him a reason. Maybe he'd go for a plea bargain.

Ernie smiled. "You'll hear from me the second I come up with anything."

"I know. Thanks."

An hour later Caige was shown into a room where Ron Seeward sat on a chair in hand and ankle cuffs. A mutinous expression altered his regular features. "I'm not talking to anyone without my attorney present."

Caige studied him for a minute. "I'm not here to discuss your case."

The other man scowled. "Then what in the hell do you want?"

Taking a plunge that might lead nowhere Caige said, "Did you take Janie away from Rick, or did he take her away from you?"

"I don't know what the hell you're talking about." Even though he'd come out with the quick answer, Caige saw something flash in his eyes.

"You don't remember him driving a bombshell brunette like her around in that flashy black BMW? Come on. You knew he was leading a double life with a false name. We have an eyewitness in San Diego who will testify under oath you and Danny knew her. Tell me what I want to know, and maybe I can help work out a deal for you."

"I had nothing to do with either of them, I tell you. Rick was one of Danny's suck-ups who was a lousy golfer and no friend of mine. All I know is, she was Rick's wife."

Wife?

Bingo, bingo, bingo.

"Thanks for your cooperation, Seeward."

Twenty minutes later Caige raced back into Mac's office. The older man looked up. "That was fast. You only have that look in your eye when you're about ready to go in for the kill."

Caige nodded. "I know Rick's last name," he said, out of breath. "It's *Pettigrew*."

Mac's razor-sharp brain put all the pieces together before he picked up the phone. "Ernie? Come to my office on the double. Caige just got back from the jail. The Farley case has cracked wide open. This is going to do it. Be prepared to roll up your sleeves."

BLAIRE RUSHED AROUND HER bedroom putting on the finishing touches. After leaving Caige's house, she'd hurried to the mall to find a new outfit to wear to the ballet, and she didn't have a lot of time to spare.

When she'd explained what she wanted, the saleswoman brought out the perfect black dress. "This calf-length chiffon has a jewel choker and mesh-illusion sleeve. With your hair and coloring, it will be stunning on you."

Once Blaire saw herself in the dressing-room mirror,

she knew this was the right dress, and she hoped it would raise Caige's blood pressure. She would wear her new black sandals with it. In her closet at home, she had a lightweight black coat with a belt that would look good.

The sound of the doorbell knocked her heart out of rhythm. She grabbed her coat and black clutch. Not needing anything else, she rushed down the stairs.

Silence greeted her after she opened the door. It came from both parties. While she was dazzled by Caige's attire—a dark blue dress suit and tie—he appeared equally taken with her. His gaze wandered over her bared shoulders and arms veiled by the sheerest chiffon, before it settled on her mouth wearing blush-peach lipstick, another purchase made before leaving the mall.

Only the sound of him taking a quick breath reached her ears. "I don't know if I dare take you out in public tonight. Maybe I should keep you to myself. *Beautiful* doesn't begin to describe how you look."

She'd already felt feverish thinking about him while she was getting dressed. "You're pretty eye-catching yourself, Ranger Dawson." He'd been just as spectacular as Jack Lignell in his forest-service uniform, but she didn't dare tell him that. She'd made a pact to keep everything professional and he'd been adhering to it.

He took her coat and helped her into it. She felt his reluctance to let go of her arms before he led her outside and pulled the door shut. After making sure it was locked, he walked her along the path to his car. Soon they were on their way.

"This is a thrill for me."

"For me, too," Caige murmured, but as they headed south, she sensed he was preoccupied.

"Was it hard for Josh to see you leave this evening?"

Caige darted her a surprised glance. "By now you know he never likes it, but he gets over it."

She clasped her purse tighter. "I'm worried he's going to look for Elly after she's gone."

They turned onto Riverside. "Don't borrow trouble, Blaire. We'll both be there for him."

"I'm probably the one who'll have the hardest time adjusting. The way she handles him, it seems second nature to her."

"Not in the beginning," he reminded her. He reached over and grasped her left hand to squeeze it before letting go. His touch shot warmth through her body. "Josh has been around you for the last three days and not one tantrum from him so far."

"I'm grateful for that."

"Tonight let's forget everything and enjoy this rare evening out." Quiet reigned until he eventually turned into the Palmer Center garage to park and they made their way over to the Long Center to watch the performance.

"Blaire?" a female voice called to her as they were walking down the aisle. She looked back.

"Irene—" The blonde woman was the mother of two of Blaire's best former piano students. She hurried toward Blaire and gave her a hug. "I thought it was you." They both smiled. "You look stunning."

Anything was a change from five years ago when Blaire had felt and looked like a battlefield victim.

Irene's eyes asked questions about Nate, but she only whispered, "Who's that gorgeous man who can't take his eyes off you?"

"A friend." She introduced them. "Uh-oh. The house-lights are dimming. I'll call you."

"Please do."

At least a dozen people in the audience who'd known her waved to her before Caige found their row. The women had caught sight of him. They were the ones who couldn't keep their eyes off *him*.

While he helped her off with her coat, he put his lips close to her ear. "This is like old home week for you."

"As I told you before, I was once a regular symphony-goer."

After they'd taken their seats, he folded her coat on his lap. The orchestra conductor took the podium. After the clapping subsided, the ballet began and the music swept her away. She thought the orchestra had never sounded better.

When the Sugar Plum Fairy came out on stage, Caige clasped her hand. "The other night when you were at the piano with Josh, you reminded me of her," he whispered. "Sparkling and magical."

Though she'd been to at least twenty performances of the *Nutcracker* in her life, with those words coming from Caige the ballet took on new enchantment for her. Every so often she gave him a covert glance. Toward the end of the performance she noticed a new expression cross over his handsome face. Whether it was pain or sadness, she couldn't say.

She imagined he was thinking of all Josh was missing and all his boy would miss growing up. A lot of parents had brought their children here tonight to enjoy the rare Christmas treat together. "In the next few years Josh could improve enough that you might be able to bring him to the *Nutcracker,*" she whispered.

"Maybe." He pressed her hand once more before relinquishing it.

Blaire decided he'd been here before with his ex-wife and it had brought back memories. Yet the more she thought about it, she decided his mood had everything to do with the changes taking place in his life. Elly would be gone on Monday, and he was giving up his career as a Texas Ranger.

You didn't do something like that unless you had absolutely no other choice on earth. Or unless you valued something else more.

That would be his Josh. The worth of a child. Beyond rubies, as the saying went.

After five curtain calls and shouts of "Bravo" for the superb performances of the lead dancers and the orchestra, Caige helped her from her seat and they made their way out of the concert hall to the car.

Neither of them seemed inclined to do much talking. They made desultory conversation but mainly drove back to her town house in companionable silence. That suited Blaire, who was deep in her own thoughts. When he pulled in the guest parking stall, she'd made up her mind that they'd say good-night at her front door.

Tomorrow she and Elly had planned for her to be at Caige's house by six-thirty. Blaire needed to see what a Saturday was like for Josh from the moment he woke up in the morning until he went to bed.

There'd be no school to take up part of the day. This would be a new test for Blaire. Caige was probably holding his breath wondering if she'd even make it through a whole twelve hours without telling him she'd changed her mind. Though she would never do that to him, he didn't know that beyond a doubt. The solemn way he looked at her after turning off the motor actually reinforced her thoughts.

"Thank you for going with me," he spoke first. "I had one of the most pleasurable evenings in years."

"So did I. Now tell me what's going on to make you look—" She paused, trying to choose her words carefully. "To make you look like you're carrying the weight of the world on your shoulders. You can tell me the truth. We've bared our souls to each other."

A tiny nerve throbbed at his temple.

"If you're having second thoughts about me taking care of Josh, then just say so. I'll understand, and I'll help you find someone who's professionally trained. You won't hurt my feelings. I promise."

"Blaire—"

"Let me finish," she interrupted him. "Tonight while I was looking at the families seated around us, it brought home once again how beloved Josh is to you. It must be so hard to trust anyone else with him. You think I don't know that?"

As her voice rang in the confines of his car, he made a strange sound and levered himself from the car in a surprise move. She quickly climbed out, fearful of what was wrong. They made their way to her front door. After she unlocked it, he followed her inside and shut it.

"Let's sit down to talk." He helped her off with her coat, but this time his hands didn't shape her arms as they had done before.

She sank down on the couch. Her heart was thudding so hard, she was afraid he could feel it even from the distance separating them. Caige pulled one of the leather chairs around so it was facing her. He sat forward with his hands clasped between his knees. "I wanted you to hear this from me first. Tomorrow morning it's going to be all over the news that Danny Dunn's case has been solved."

Her eyes widened in disbelief. *"Solved?"* Out of all the reasons she'd come up with tonight for Caige's change of mood, the Danny Dunn case hadn't been one of them. Shaken by the news, she got up from the couch, unable to remain seated. "Who killed him?"

Caige gave her a frank stare. "He was shot by his lover, Charlie Beck. It happened in Ron Seeward's house. He's in custody and has made a full confession."

For the next few minutes she listened spellbound while Caige told her everything. She took several unsteady breaths after he'd finished. "So there's nothing to implicate Nate in any of this?"

"No."

"Neither Ron Seeward or Charlie Beck knows anything about his disappearance?"

"I'm sorry, Blaire."

She turned away from him, dry-eyed. "I'm sorry, too.

He really did vanish into thin air. Naturally I'm glad he didn't have anything to do with Mr. Dunn's death, but it feels as though a door has been slammed shut forever."

Suddenly Caige wrapped his arms around her from behind, pressing his face against her hair. "Don't despair. Clearing up the Dunn case makes my hunt for your husband that much easier."

Blaire whirled around, grasping his upper arms. "How can you say that?"

"Because all of this time I've been following up on other leads. An investigation goes step by step. Sometimes one lead takes off on a detour, but there's always another one that brings you closer."

"So you have other viable leads at this point?" Her blue eyes implored him for answers.

"Yes. Several. For the next week I'm going to be busier than ever. To know you'll be home taking care of Josh relieves my mind more than you know. Now I can really concentrate."

She searched his eyes. "Do you honestly believe you'll find out what happened to him?"

"I can tell you this much with all the honesty in me. I'll never give up trying. How about a kiss for luck? Otherwise I might die for the wanting."

His husky voice seduced her so completely, she forgot the rules and threw her arms around his neck. This time no chaste kiss touched her lips and was gone again. Caige kissed her as if he'd been hungering for this a long time. She opened her mouth to him, experiencing rapture as their bodies came together in need. The passion flaring between them was like a slow-burning fire growing so hot it was enveloping them.

He carried her over to the couch and pressed her back against the pillows. For the next little while he kissed every inch of her face and throat, inducing tiny moans of pleasure from her.

"I've been wanting to do this for so long," he confessed on a ragged breath. "Sometimes in the trees I've seen the way the sunlight dapples your hair and skin. It's so soft and creamy. And your mouth. I've been dying for a taste of it, but now I find this isn't enough. Your dress has driven me mad all night." As if to prove it, he kissed the bare skin showing through the chiffon.

"I want to take you to bed. The first time you jumped down from the tree I wanted you. Help me to stay away from you until I find out what happened to Nate. Don't let me get this close again. I don't want you to be confused when I make love to you for the first time."

She'd twined her fingers in his hair. "What do you mean? I'm not confused."

He gave her one more hot kiss, then got to his feet and stood over her. "Maybe not right this minute. But when you wake up tomorrow, you might feel I took advantage of you."

Blaire had been so enthralled with their lovemaking, his comment didn't register at first. When it did, she eased up on her elbows. "I would *never* think that. If anything, it's the other way around. You know something, don't you?" He didn't look away. In fact, he did nothing, but she wasn't reassured.

After sitting up, she got off the couch, albeit unsteadily, and smoothed the hair he'd mussed from her face. "Why do I sense there's more to this?"

Caige put his hands on his hips. "With the other case solved, I have hopes we're much closer to solving yours now."

Was he worried that she wouldn't feel the same way about him if or when he discovered what had happened to Nate? Caige had no idea how much she loved him. Her body was still clamoring for his kisses.

I don't want you to be confused when I make love to you for the first time.

Needing to believe that day would come and they'd make glorious love forever and ever, she drew from all the strength within her and moved to the entry. "It was a heavenly evening." She opened the door. "I'll see you tomorrow."

He eyed her swollen lips through veiled lashes. "Good night."

"Good night."

She locked the door after him and hurried upstairs to bed, reliving those moments in his arms when he'd carried her to the couch. He'd set her on fire and it would never go out. She knew she'd still be burning up at six-thirty in the morning when she needed to be at his house.

BLAIRE REACHED FOR JOSH'S hand. "Come on, sweetheart. Let's go home."

Elly had sat in her car reading a book while she was waiting for them. They'd driven to a nearby park after Josh's lunch. The weather was still in the sixties and they were both comfortable wearing jackets. She'd put sunscreen on his face to protect him.

Armed with a ball and some cars, Blaire had played with him for a couple of hours. He'd loved his snacks and had drunk from the water bottle Elly had brought along. It had been a pleasant afternoon with other children around playing. Josh occasionally lifted his head when he heard someone shouting, but for the most part he remained in his world.

She gathered the bag with his things in one hand and they started walking. Or at least *she* tried taking a step, but Josh pulled back and sat down. At first she thought he might have stumbled, and she urged him to get up again, but he refused.

After putting the bag back down, she knelt in front of him. "Don't you want to go?"

Tears filled his eyes, terrifying her. She sat down by him and handed him a car. He clutched it with both hands, touching the different parts as he'd been doing on and off while they'd been there. Five minutes later she put the car back in the bag and stood up. "Come on. Let's go." Once again she reached for him. Josh wouldn't get up, and more tears filled his eyes.

This was what she presumed was a tantrum. She hadn't seen him do this before. On Thursday night she'd read some medical information online that said tantrums in children like Josh could last a long or a short time. Sometimes it was a waiting game. One article said that if you distracted a child with something they wanted, they might snap out of it, but Blaire didn't have anything on her. She'd left her purse in the car with Elly.

Out of desperation, she pulled some more snacks out of the bag. After putting them in her palm, she extended her hand to him. He liked that. Into his mouth they went. A new game. She did it a few more times. "These are good, huh?"

Their faces were close. Suddenly he kissed her cheek three times. Little angel pecks that caught at her heart.

She kissed him the same way. Without saying any words, she held his hand and got up. To her joy, he stood up and they walked to the car. Elly had gotten out and was waiting for them with a smile.

"Tantrum over?"

"Yes." Blaire was so relieved, they both chuckled before she fastened Josh in the backseat. When they drove home, Caige, dressed in jeans and a polo shirt, came out the front door and made a beeline for his son.

"Hey, buddy. You were gone so long, you must have had a great time." Josh always clung to his father.

Elly nodded. "We certainly did."

"We would have been home ten minutes sooner, but he didn't want to leave," Blaire explained. "I just played with him some more and then gave him a few more snacks. It seemed to do the trick."

"And she was rewarded with kisses." Elly winked at Blaire, who hadn't realized she'd been watched that closely.

Caige flashed Blaire a half smile that set off butterflies in her stomach. "Kisses mean he's happy."

"I kissed him back."

"Lucky him," he murmured before walking him in the house. When they reached the hallway he turned to

Elly. "Do you mind starting his bath without Blaire? I only need to talk to her for a minute."

"No problem. Come on, Josh. Let's get you all cleaned up."

Blaire noticed him hang on to his father, but he finally let go and went with Elly to his bathroom.

"We'll go in my den." She followed Caige into his inner sanctum with its wall of books. He kept pictures of his family and Josh in here. There were other pictures of him in his younger days with some of his colleagues. Blaire had no doubt he had photos of his ex-wife. Maybe he'd stored them in a box or a drawer.

She sat down in one of the wingback chairs. He perched on the corner of his desk that held his computer.

"While you were gone this afternoon, I was tracing down another lead. It turns out I'm going to have to go out of town tomorrow. If I fly out early in the morning, I can be back by evening. I hadn't anticipated leaving you this soon, but it's vital."

It had to be for him to consider such a move.

"Since tomorrow is Elly's last day, you still have her for backup while she packs. But if, heaven forbid, I can't get back until Monday morning, how do you feel about being on your own this soon?"

"Caige—don't worry about me. I'm getting more and more comfortable with Josh all the time. To be honest, I'm glad I experienced one of his tantrums today. We got past it, and that gives me more confidence."

He wore a concerned expression. "If you have any doubts, I could put this off until next—"

"Please don't," she broke in on him. "This is exactly

why I told you I wanted to take care of Josh. You need to act immediately on any information you find. Every time you have to leave, I know it's because you're working on my case. What time do you need me?"

"Six in the morning."

"I'll be here." She got up from the chair. "If that's everything, I'm going to go see how Josh is doing."

"Blaire? I'll only be a phone call away. Elly has already shown you that list of phone numbers we keep in the kitchen. The doctors, Gracie, my parents and family, my boss and his wife. All of them have helped with Josh at one time or other."

"That's good to know."

He nodded. "After his bath, I'm going to take all of us for a ride out to Travis Lake. I thought it would be nice to have a goodbye dinner for Elly. I've got some presents for her."

"I bought her one, too, but I'll have to give it to her tomorrow."

"She'll appreciate that. In case you didn't know, she thinks the world of you."

"I think the same of her, but she hardly knows me."

"It's your way with Josh that has impressed her. The way it has me," he added in his deep voice.

"I won't let you down."

Blaire hurried out of the den and down the hall to the bathroom. She took over for Elly, knowing what to do because she'd already bathed and dressed Josh three times this week. "Let me do this while you get ready."

Elly smiled. "For what?"

"Just trust me."

An hour later the four of them took off in the car in a festive mood. Caige explained that Josh loved going through the drive-through car wash, so they did. Josh rocked back and forth in his seat, obviously excited while the water squirted over the car.

Blaire sat in the backseat with him and had strapped him in. He smelled so sweet and seemed so eager, she gave him several kisses. On the drive home, she reached over and slipped her fingers into his right hand, not knowing if he would reject her or not. The gesture was impulsive on her part because she was so thrilled to be out with Caige and his son.

When his fingers curled around hers and hung on tightly, she could have cried for happiness. As she lifted her head, her gaze met Caige's silvery gaze through the rearview mirror. The tender look in them constituted one of the supreme moments of her life.

Chapter Ten

Caige landed at the San Diego airport at ten o'clock Sunday morning under overcast skies. Thanks to Ernie, who had finally got hold of the former manager of the Sterling Luxury Condos in La Jolla, he had a definite destination in mind. Everything ten his gut told him he was on the verge of a discovery that could end Blaire's nightmare. Though he was going on information that was more than five years old, he felt this lead held the key.

Following the directions on the GPS navigator, he drove his rental car north on I-5. At three miles he took Greenways Vista Road and headed west until he came to the entrance to the Mourning Dove Golf and Country Club Complex. According to Ernie, it was worth $250,000,000 on today's market, if you include the course itself, the clubhouse, shops and the twenty-four luxury homes surrounding the fairway.

He read the sign:

Welcome to Mourning Dove, home of world-acclaimed golf-course designer and architect

Creed Marshall III, named premier golfing architect by *Hole-In-One Monthly*.

Though not a golf enthusiast, Caige had watched segments of the various PGA specials on TV over the years and had admired the beauty of the unique landscaping that made up a famous golf course. But nothing had prepared him for the sight before him.

The cliffside fairways looked out over the blue Pacific. Sloping velvety greens hugged the rugged coastline. A limited number of fabulous homes with red-tiled roofs lined the concourses. For the megamillionaires who lived and died for golf, this had to be paradise.

While driving through to the country club in the distance, he passed a stable and tennis courts. Farther on, he caught a glimpse of the Olympic-size swimming pool. This had it all. He eventually parked the car in the front courtyard and entered the rambling structure. It reflected a mixture of its Native American roots and Spanish-mission heritage.

A sign indicated the general offices were reached by a colorful hand-painted-tile staircase edged with flowers spilling over their terra-cotta pots. It rose to the next level, dominating the west portion of the foyer.

Signed photographs of the most renowned golfers in the world had been framed and mounted on the stucco walls. Many of them paid tribute to Creed Marshall's genius.

The golf and pro shops were at the other end of the building. Before he talked to the management, he walked around to familiarize himself with the floor plan. He came to the crowded golf shop filled with all the golfing necessities known to man. It looked like the interior of the most upscale department store. Caige zeroed in on the three employees waiting on customers. Two of them were good-looking women who wore the shop's latest golf apparel.

After a few minutes he headed into the pro shop with its training aids and bookstore. In one section you could watch videos. There was a nook where you could buy and sell used golf clubs. He walked over to the area of the room devoted to a setup of the home practice center. One of the upbeat male employees approached him with a smile. He'd dressed in a trendy outfit for the golfer who wanted to be noticed.

"What can I help you out with today? If you're wanting to improve your game, this can really help."

Caige turned to him. "I was just looking."

"Great. Take all the time you want. If you need anything, come and find me."

"Thank you."

In another minute he left the shop and walked down to the other end of the long hall filled with potted trees and plants. The restaurant was filled by the Sunday brunch crowd. According to the board outside the entrance, the fresh catch of the day was swordfish. There were conference rooms farther on.

The maître d' gave him a polite smile. "Welcome to the Dove Creek restaurant. I'm Agosto. Are you dining alone or expecting someone?" He spoke with a slight Italian accent.

"Actually, I'm looking for Richard Pettigrew. Someone told me he worked here as a sous-chef." The lie was worth a shot.

The man darted him a puzzled glance. "If you mean Rick, he's Mr. Marshall's son-in-law and works upstairs."

Caige shook his head. "The Richard I'm looking for goes by Dick and is divorced. We're obviously talking about the wrong person here. He's five-eight. Black hair. Wiry."

"Rick is dark blond and married with two children."

"My mistake. It seems I was definitely given the wrong information. Sorry." There were people waiting in line behind him.

"No problem."

"Thank you."

Struggling to keep himself from letting out a victory yell heard round the world, Caige retraced his steps and climbed the staircase to the next level. There were nameplates on three different doors. Bob McKay, President. Bruce Marshall, Vice President. Would that be a son, a brother, an uncle or the father of Creed Marshall?

Caige's gaze flicked to the third door. Rick Pettigrew, Assistant Director.

He left the club and hurried out to the parking lot. Once behind the wheel of the car, he pulled out his phone and called Mac. He answered on the third ring.

"Hate to bother you on your day off, Mac, but I've hit pay dirt."

"Is Farley alive or dead?"

Though part of him felt incredible elation, the part that would have to tell Blaire the news caused him to grimace. "Very much alive. He has two children. There's a special spot reserved for the management out here in the parking area. I see a Ferrari, a Porsche and a Maserati. I'm going to sit here until I get a visual on him and take a picture."

An eloquent silence followed. "The second you get it, I'll call Tim Robbins. He'll want to coordinate a sting operation."

"While you do that, I'll start Ernie working on a complete background check."

"I'll get back to you. Have I ever told you Ranger Dawson does great work? Don't you leave us!"

Caige would have liked to reassure him, but too many things were up in the air right now.

Once Mac had hung up, Caige made the call to Ernie, who let out a bark of excitement so loud it hurt his eardrum. While they spoke, he started up the car and drove as close as he dared to the luxury cars. He needed to get good pictures.

This being a Sunday, Caige figured the lowlife wouldn't stick around all day. The clock said eleven-thirty. He had to be at the airport by five-thirty. Luckily it wasn't more than a half hour away if you factored in traffic.

For the next two hours he spoke on and off to his colleagues, discussing strategies. He'd bought diet colas and Milky Way bars on the way to Mourning Dove. They would have to do for his lunch because he wasn't moving from the spot.

Agent Robbins phoned him. All he needed was a positive ID, then they'd decide on a plan of attack.

He checked in on Blaire. "How's it going?"

"Fine. Josh has eaten most of his peanut-butter sandwich. When he's finished, I'll drive him to the park. I told Elly not to come with us. She's got a dozen things to attend to, but she keeps stopping to give Josh a hug. She's going to miss him."

"I have no doubt of it, but when she's back with her sister, she'll have freedom she hasn't enjoyed in over a year."

"You're right." After a pause she said, "Are you okay?"

"Busy."

"Then I won't keep you." She didn't ask him more questions. Good, because he wouldn't have answered them.

"I could be home by as early as nine this evening. Otherwise it will have to be tomorrow morning."

"Understood. Don't you worry about anything here. We're terrific."

He bowed his head. All that was going to change within twenty-four hours. "Take care, Blaire."

"You, too."

They clicked off. Caige checked his watch. Ten after two. When he lifted his head, there was Nathan Farley, coming out the doors of the building big as life. Caige started snapping pictures.

What was it Ernie had said the owner of the shooting range had told him? *They came several times in a black BMW convertible in their flashy clothes. He thought they might be film stars because he was good-*

looking and had that kind of tan you don't get in the States.

One of these days Caige would drive out to that shooting range with Blaire and they'd thank Mel for the tip that helped him put the bits and pieces together.

He followed Farley at a discreet distance. Relying on his binoculars, he watched the car pull into the garage of one of the hacienda-type houses along Mourning Dove Way. It reeked of money.

Once the door closed, he drove by and snapped more pictures. On his way to the airport he phoned Agent Robbins. "You've got your proof. I downloaded it and just pressed Send."

"I'm looking for it right now." Caige didn't have to wait long for the response. Robbins's whistle came close to damaging his other eardrum. "The Koslov family is going to get their long-awaited Christmas present. How do you want to handle it with Blaire?"

Caige drew in a sharp breath. "She's going to want to confront him. Let's let her do it in his office."

"He'll have a gun on him and possibly one in the drawer."

"Yup. We'll go in first to arrest and cuff him. Then we'll leave her alone with him."

"I'll set it up with the feds in California so that when they're through with him, we can extradite him to Texas for trial."

Caige gripped his phone tighter. "We need to move as fast as possible. This close to Christmas, I don't want to take any chances he might be leaving for somewhere else and we miss nabbing him."

"We'll do it tomorrow."

Caige wanted to take Farley into custody right now. "Perfect."

ELLY LEFT CAIGE'S HOUSE at seven while Josh was taking his bath. After more hugs and promises to keep in touch, Blaire found herself alone with Josh. With Caige out of the house, too, his son was a great comfort to her.

Josh didn't react to Elly's leaving. She wondered how long it would be before he started missing Elly. An hour, a day? She was thankful he was being so good. At eight she started the ritual of putting him to bed. First came the pull-up diaper and his pajamas. Then the teeth-brushing. That took some time because he thought it was a game. Finally he lay down cuddling an old blue bunny.

The darling fell asleep fast. Caige told her that once Josh's head touched the pillow, he faded quickly. That is unless he had a cold and grew restless. Such a day was bound to come soon, but not tonight, thank heaven.

Elly had changed the sheets on her bed and scoured her bathroom. Everything was ready for Blaire to take over. The sunny room with its yellow-and-white motif had once been a guest bedroom. Caige's ex-wife's great decorating sense was reflected throughout the house.

With her phone stashed in her jeans pocket, Blaire looked in on Josh one more time before going in the kitchen to watch TV. Nothing held her interest. She surfed channels. At nine Caige phoned. After saying hello, she held her breath, wondering if he'd been detained.

"Just so you know, I'm driving home from the airport and should be there in five minutes."

Her heart clapped so hard she was certain he'd heard it. "Good. Josh is asleep. I'm free to fix you a meal if you're hungry."

"Thanks, but I stopped for a sandwich. Did Elly get off all right?"

"Yes. At seven."

"Don't go to bed yet, Blaire. We have to talk."

He clicked off too fast for her to respond. While she was watching news on cable without taking any of it in, she heard the garage door open. In a second his tall, well-honed body entered the kitchen through the other door.

"Hi," she said and turned off the TV.

His gaze swept over her with new urgency. "Hi yourself."

They stood facing each other, almost as if they were adversaries. He was in a white knit shirt and jeans. She was wearing one of her Trees for Life T-shirts. Nerves caused her stomach muscles to clench. "Is it good news or bad?"

"Let's sit down first."

She did his bidding, but she couldn't stand the waiting. "Just tell me the truth. After this long I can take anything."

Caige sank down on one of the chairs. "He's alive," he ground out.

Her right hand gripped the edge of the table. "You *saw* him?"

"Yes."

Blaire twisted out of her chair in shock. Suddenly her life was flashing before her. *Nate wasn't dead....* She'd honestly been prepared for the news that he was. But for him to be alive—

"Where did you see him?" she demanded.

"In La Jolla, California."

She frowned. "Has he been in a hospital all this time with amnesia or something?"

"Come here." He pulled her onto his lap, wrapping his arms around her waist. His strong legs cradled hers. "Let me tell you what I know for a fact. The rest we'll learn tomorrow when you and I fly to San Diego and you confront Nate yourself."

Confront meant that her husband was capable of being confronted. All the moisture in her mouth dried up. She felt Caige's arms tighten in a protective gesture.

After kissing her temple he said, "He goes by the name Rick Pettigrew and is married to a woman named Janie Marshall. Her father, Creed Marshall, is the famous golf-course architect who designed the multimillion-dollar Mourning Dove Golf and Country Club Complex in La Jolla. Rick drives a Ferrari and is an assistant director. He lives in one of the homes on the estate there bordering the golf course. They have two children."

AGENT ROBBINS MET THEM at the plane in San Diego. He turned around as Blaire climbed in the back of the unmarked car with Caige. "Remember me?"

"Of course. You were always kind to me."

"I always wanted to believe in your innocence."

"That's what my mother told me. It's why she and Dad approached you a few weeks ago."

He flashed her a quick smile. "There was only one man in the State of Texas who Mac Leesom told me we could turn to in order to solve your case."

She nodded. Blaire owed a debt of gratitude to a certain Texas Ranger she could never repay, but right now she had only one thing on her mind. "Is the country club very far from here?"

"Twenty minutes." He started the car and they left to get on the freeway headed north. "Our task team is on the premises undercover, ready to act. Caige will make the arrest. When Mr. Farley can't be a danger to anyone, we'll let you have your time alone with your husband."

"He's not *my* husband," she said in a wintry tone. "I never knew that man."

"Mrs. Pettigrew will be saying the same thing in another few hours. Bigamy in the state of California brings at least a one-year prison sentence and a ten-thousand-dollar fine. In Texas it can bring up to a ten-year prison sentence with the same fine. His problems don't end there.

"After Caige interrogated Ron Seeward, the caddy broke down and implicated your husband in a money-laundering scheme that involved Danny Dunn. He did it hoping for a plea bargain."

Blaire shivered.

"The U.S. Attorney's Office's Asset Forfeiture Division has filed a civil forfeiture complaint in connection with the seizure of more than $70,000 in cash and the BMW bought by your husband. It was purchased with the proceeds of the illegal operation in a structured fashion to avoid the financial-transaction-reporting requirements."

What she was hearing now sounded like pure fiction, but she knew it wasn't. Nate was capable of anything.

"A maximum penalty for violation of the money-laundering statute can be up to twenty years in prison and a $250,000 fine, while the conspiracy and structuring charges each carry a maximum term of imprisonment of up to five years and a $250,000 fine. With a possibility of facing thirty-six years behind bars, he's in serious trouble, Blaire."

She stared out the window, completely numb.

A bigamist involved in money laundering.

The answer for his disappearance was as simple as that, and as complex, especially when she thought about his other wife and children, who were innocent. Their grief lay ahead of them. Caige found her hand, twining his fingers through hers the way Josh had done. Any life beating inside her right now beat for them.

She looked at Caige. "Does he know you know anything yet?"

"No. We'll be taking him by complete surprise."

"When he disappeared, it took *me* by complete surprise."

When the car stopped, she heard officers talking over the car radio. Agent Robbins let the team of men know they'd arrived. She stepped out into sixty-four-degree weather, only a few degrees warmer than Austin, and looked around. The setting of the swank country club and the fancy cars dotting the parking lot were *sooo* Nate.

Caige studied her frozen features. "Are you ready, or do you need more time?"

Her gaze met his head-on. "I don't intend to waste another millisecond on that man than I have to."

His jaw hardened. "Then let's go."

She walked between the two men. They entered the country club and headed for the staircase. Nate's eyes had to have popped out of his head when he first saw this place. He'd been living the dream for a long time, and dreaming the dream long before that—probably since he was out at the old municipal golf course mowing lawns at sixteen.

They passed a man on the stairs. There were more in the hallway upstairs. Anyone around would think they were people doing business with the management. Three of them eyed Caige. He sent her a final glance before they entered the door bearing Rick Pettigrew's name.

It couldn't have been ten seconds later when one of them came out with a frightened-looking woman, probably the secretary, who wanted to know what was going on. The officer walked her down the stairs out of earshot.

Agent Robbins sent Blaire a smile of support. When she didn't think she could stand it another second, he answered his phone, then gave her a nod. Taking courage in her hands, she headed for the door and walked inside. The two officers and Caige, whose features were masklike, had placed themselves outside the inner suite. His gray eyes sent the message she could go on in.

Blaire stepped inside. Nothing about Nate's office looked disturbed or out of place except for Nate himself. Caige had seated him on what looked like the secretary's swivel chair in the middle of the room. He faced his own desk. His arms had been pulled behind him with his wrists handcuffed. She noticed his ankles were cuffed.

Blaire let out the deep breath she'd been holding. "Hello, Nate."

He recognized her voice, of course. It took several minutes before he worked himself around with his bound ankles to look at her. His gaze swept over her, taking in the red lapelled jacket and black pants she'd worn the wonderful night she and Caige had decorated his Christmas tree.

She had to admit the past five years had been kind to the man she'd once loved. His hair was lighter because of the hours spent under the sun. The bronze of his tan had never been more becoming. Blue-eyed, attractive. He wore expensive designer clothes and shoes.

Blaire walked around him. On his ring finger he wore a wedding band with a sapphire. His nails looked so perfect, she suspected he'd had a manicure recently. A nice cologne that didn't smell familiar permeated the room. But for the restraints, he would look the epitome of success. But she wondered how good it truly tasted, since he hadn't reached the rank of a pro golfer and was living on his father-in-law's money.

A few more steps and she was facing him again. "You're a pretty man, Nate. You've hardly aged over the years. I don't see the normal lines of experience around your mouth, or the expected creases in your forehead. No gray at your temples yet. Not even laughter lines at the sides of your eyes. It's because there's nothing behind the facade that makes you real."

"Blaire—"

"I don't want to know when you met Janie, or whether you married her before or after you married me. In fact, I don't know if you were married to someone else before both of us, or if you're carrying on with still another woman right now and Janie doesn't know about it yet."

"You don't understand," he muttered.

"No one understands a sociopath." He flinched. "None of it matters. I'm only here for one reason. They say it's good for your mental health to be able to see the body after someone dies. I've finally been granted that blessing." Thanks to the most remarkable, noble man on earth. "Rest in peace, *whoever* you are."

As she turned to leave, Nate unexpectedly screamed her name in a bloodcurdling voice. Everyone in the country club would have heard it. He shouted for her to come back, begged her, before he broke down sobbing.

She kept walking until she reached the outer hall where Caige was waiting for her with the other officers. His compassionate gray eyes were filled with pain for her. That was the kind of man he was.

Agent Robbins approached her. "Do you think you're going to want any more time with him before he's taken to jail?"

"No. Do you need me to do anything or sign anything?"

"Not until after we're back in Texas and you feel up to it."

She stared at Caige. "Then I want to go home."

Nate's sobs followed them as Caige cupped her elbow and they walked down the stairs. Outside the club he gripped her around the shoulders and pulled her hard against the side of his warm, solid body while they made their way to the parking lot.

When they reached the car, he helped her into the backseat. No words were necessary as he drew her into his arms and they both held each other tight. Tears leaked from her eyes onto his neck. "It's over. This whole hideous nightmare is over," she cried. "Thank God for you, Caige."

The drive passed in a blur as Agent Robbins drove them back to the San Diego airport. Cocooned by Caige, she hardly remembered the flight back to Austin, or the drive through the city. She'd been in such a daze, reality didn't hit her until she realized he'd pulled up in the driveway of her parents' home.

She blinked before jerking her head toward him. "What are we doing here?"

"I talked with your parents earlier. They asked me to bring you home. I promised them I'd do it."

Panic gripped her. Naturally she was anxious to see her parents and tell them everything, but she didn't want to be away from Caige tonight. "I'll call them on the way to your house."

"Plans have changed, Blaire."

She felt a sharp, jabbing pain. "What do you mean?"

"While you have a much-needed reunion with your family, Josh and I need one with mine. I'm following my sister back to Naylor tonight. Your car is safe in my driveway until your father takes you over to get it tomorrow."

When he'd brought her back from San Diego, she didn't know she'd be fighting for her life as soon as they touched the ground. "I don't understand. I agreed to take care of Josh."

"That's true, but your case has been solved. I don't have any more work, and I need a break. Under the circumstances I'm going to close up the house and take Josh to Naylor for the holidays."

Nooo!

"There'll be plenty of family around to help me. After talking to your folks, I sensed they need you very badly. These last five years must have been ghastly for them, too. You should have heard their joy when I told them the news."

She bowed her head. "I know it took years off their lives."

"I'd like to think this news has put some of them back on."

"I would, too, Caige." She struggled for breath. Naturally he needed a break. All he'd done was work night and day to solve her case. But now that it was behind them, she'd thought…

Don't beg, Blaire. Don't ever beg.

"How do I begin to thank you?" Her voice trembled.

"By getting back in touch with yourself. You're a free

woman now with the rest of your life ahead of you. Over the years I've seen enough in my job to know that when a person who's been under siege is finally released, they have to rediscover who they really are. Often their minds won't allow them to do that for a while."

I know who I am, Caige Dawson.

To her chagrin she had the sinking feeling he was the one who'd gotten too close to the situation and was trying to back off without hurting her feelings. It probably happened more often than not in his kind of work. A lot of forced togetherness produced a bond, but it ended when there was no more reason for it.

She'd been the one to ask for the job of tending Josh, not the other way around. When he'd said he needed a break, she was pretty sure he'd meant a break from her. Blaire knew he liked her. Their desire for each other had been real enough, but desire didn't necessarily translate to something more permanent.

If she didn't want to ruin any hope of being with him in the future, it looked like she was going to have to let him pick the pace of their relationship, *if* he desired one at a later date. For the time being he wanted a separation.

Was it to get back in touch with himself? If so, then she knew to give him his space.

While she sat there in fresh agony, she heard voices, including her sister's. The family had heard them drive up and had rushed outside to greet them. One nightmare had ended…

But a brand-new one had begun.

Chapter Eleven

"Dr. Sweeney? Thanks for getting back to me. I wouldn't have bothered you the day before Christmas if I weren't alarmed over Josh."

"My service said this was urgent. What's wrong with him?"

"Since I brought him to Naylor three days ago, he's changed and won't let me out of his sight. Normally he interacts happily with the members of my family. So far he's pushed everyone away who comes close. He doesn't want me talking to anyone or showing attention. I can tell he doesn't like it that I'm on the phone with you. It's almost as if he's jealous."

"Does he have a fever?"

"No. His temp is normal. Physically he seems fine, and he eats for me. It's his behavior that has me disturbed. I'm in the bedroom with him right now and he's just lying here clinging to me. If I try to do anything as harmless as going into the bathroom, tears start and he comes with me. I've never seen him act like this before."

"Did he manifest this behavior before you left Austin, or after you arrived in Naylor?"

"After. We're staying at my parents' home. Tuesday

morning when he got up, he didn't act himself after we had breakfast. I brought his toys to play with, but he threw them across the floor. He wanted his cousins to go away and pushed them, only wanting me. This isn't typical of him. Do you think I need to take him to the hospital?"

"Let me ask a few more questions first. Has he never acted out like this around your family?"

"No. We were here at Thanksgiving and he was fine. In fact, he has always liked it here. This is something new."

"Is your housekeeper with you?"

"No. And she won't be anymore because she has left my employ. But she has never come on a family vacation with us, so he wouldn't know anything different while we're here."

"Did something happen at school?"

"If it had, Mrs. Wright would have told me. Since he's not riding the school bus yet, he wasn't set off by another student."

"So nothing in his world has changed? You've done nothing different?"

Caige lowered his head. Everything had changed... everything was different.... The last three days had been an eternity without seeing or talking to Blaire. Feeling utterly helpless, he stared down at his boy curled into him for dear life. He wished Josh could talk and tell him what was wrong, but that miracle wasn't going to happen.

"A woman I've been working with on a law-enforcement case has been in our lives over the last three weeks. Leading up to my housekeeper's departure, Blaire spent time with her and Josh with the understanding that she would take over after Elly left."

"Where is this Blaire now?"

He breathed deeply. "Home with her family."

And he hoped a healing process was going on for her. The psychiatrist who'd helped Caige through his trauma three years ago had told him he'd needed time to get back in touch with his real self. He'd warned him about not getting involved with another woman while he was in the grieving stage.

"Let it go through its natural cycle so it won't catch up with you later on, Caige. I've seen too many patients who tried to rush it, then don't understand why a new relationship isn't working." Looking back, the doctor's advice had made a lot of sense. Blaire was now in her grieving phase and needed to have time alone to do it.

"What was Josh's behavior like with her?"

The question brought an explosion of memories whooshing through his mind. "He accepted Blaire from the beginning. Toward the end, he let her do everything while Elly stayed in the background. He even let her clip his toenails, whereas he normally fights with me. She had a way of handling him that was so natural, I was amazed. Blaire was very loving with him."

"She may be the key."

Caige's heart skidded to a stop before taking an extra beat. "But he wasn't with her that long—"

"How old is she?"

"Twenty-nine."

"How old was your wife at the time of the accident?"

"Twenty-eight."

"Not a great difference in their ages."

He blinked. "Are you saying what I think you're saying?"

"This is only a theory, mind you, but it's possible some memory from the past has been resurrected. He lost his mother at five. Now Blaire enters the picture and suddenly she's no longer in his world. Perhaps he's missing her smell or her touch. Maybe a tone in her voice or even her energy. Something evocative from the past. I've seen it happen before."

Excitement welled up inside him. "That would mean—"

"It would mean he's capable of more cognitive thought," the doctor finished the sentence. "The human brain is a wondrous thing, but let's not get ahead of ourselves. What I propose is that before you put him in the hospital for testing, you contact Blaire and see if she can't pay Josh a visit. The experiment might or might not work. However, I believe it's worth trying."

So do I.

Caige manifested the same symptoms as his son. If he couldn't have Blaire, he didn't want anyone else. Until it was proven otherwise to him, he would go with his own gut instinct that the neuropsychologist had nailed the problem.

"I owe you thanks more than you know, Dr. Sweeney."

"You're welcome. Let me hear from you about the results."

"I will."

The second he got off the phone, he checked his watch. It was almost two in the afternoon. Blaire could be anywhere, doing anything. But Josh's life, Caige's life, depended on finding her.

BLAIRE HAD ALREADY BOUGHT all her gifts, but her dad had asked her to go with him while he finished up some last-minute Christmas shopping. It was an excuse to get her out of the house because he knew she was missing Caige so badly, she was dying.

While they were in the car, her cell phone rang for the third time. She was terrified to look at the caller ID. Every time her ring tone had gone off, she'd suffered a heart attack because it wasn't Caige. She didn't know if she could go through that again.

Over the past few days she'd had several dozen calls from old friends and coworkers who'd heard the breaking news about Nate's arrest and wanted to lend their support. Perry and Marty were particularly sweet to her. It was all over the local media how Texas Ranger Caige Dawson had cracked two cold cases that had eluded law enforcement for the past five years.

"Aren't you going to answer it?" her father asked as he pulled in the driveway.

"I'll call them back." Her phone was in her purse.

"It might be important."

"You mean it might be Caige." She shook her head. "I don't think so. He made it clear he was going home for Christmas to be with family. One of these days I'll hear from him, probably sometime in January after he's settled there with Josh. It will be in the form of a touch-base kind of call. His way of wrapping up the case for good."

Before they could open their car doors, it rang again. Her father shot her a speaking glance, then got out to get some gifts and groceries from the trunk. With a moan, she reached in her purse for the phone to retrieve the latest message. It was Caige's deep voice.

Blaire? Please call when you can. This is extremely important.

No preamble, no chitchat asking how she was. He sounded more distraught than she'd ever heard him. Frantic even. After checking the messages, she realized all three calls had been from him.

She phoned him immediately, praying for him to answer straightaway.

"Thank heaven it's you—" he blurted after the first ring. "Can you come to Naylor right now? Bring some clothes for overnight. Josh isn't dying, but there is something wrong with him. I need your help."

Blaire could hardly breathe. "I'll leave in five minutes. Where are you?"

"At my parents' home. This is the address." He gave her directions.

"I'll be there as soon as I can."

The next few minutes were a blur as she ran into the house to inform her parents of the emergency. They helped her gather the few things she'd need and brought the presents she'd bought for Caige and Josh to her car. After they hugged, she promised to call them as soon as she had news, then took off for Naylor.

While she drove the sixty miles, her mind relived

every moment of her life since Jack Lignell had helped her get up after her jump from that oak tree. He'd not only given her life back to her, he'd transformed her world. There wasn't anything she wouldn't do for him.

His parents' two-story ranch house sat back a mile from the main street. The straight dirt road leading in was lined with fencing. She spotted Nate's red Toyota parked alongside some cars and a couple of pickup trucks to the side of the house.

Two people about the ages of her parents came out to greet her and introduce themselves. She could see where Caige got his attractive looks. His parents wore anxious faces.

"Our son is in the front room with Josh. Go on in. We'll bring your things."

The fact that Caige hadn't come outside himself spoke volumes.

"Thank you."

Blaire hurried on in, not knowing what to expect. She found Caige sitting on the couch with Josh in his arms. Both were dressed in plaid shirts and jeans. The boy had buried his dark head against his father's shoulder, as if he didn't want to look at anything. What a sad irony when there was a beautiful Christmas tree dominating the living room. Caige's mother had made the place a fairyland.

When Blaire drew closer, Caige lifted his head. She saw several emotions stirring in those gray eyes staring back at her. Part pain and part something else that took her breath away.

"Thank you for coming," he whispered.

She clamped down hard not to let her feelings spill out in a gush. "I wouldn't be anyplace else, would I, Josh?" On instinct, she sat down next to them and leaned over to kiss Josh's cheek. She saw moisture on his lashes.

"Hi, sweetheart," she said with a broken heart. "It's Blaire. I've missed you." She inserted two fingers into the curled hand pressed against Caige's chest.

No response. Caige had been right. Josh was a different child from a few days ago. He'd shut out the world. If she were Caige, she'd be terrified.

After easing her fingers away, she got up and went over to the tree where his parents had put her gifts. She undid the package containing a squirrel. It had the cutest face and eyes, and it was the softest stuffed animal she could find. Blaire knew he loved his old blue bunny, but maybe he'd welcome a new pet.

She moved toward them once more. Bending over, she tickled Josh's chin with the squirrel's tail. "This is Bushy." She rubbed it back and forth along his jawline, teasing his lips and nose in the process. His darling face was a replica of his handsome father's. "Doesn't he feel good?"

Josh buried himself deeper against his father.

Caige's haunted expression devastated her. She couldn't bear that the progress she'd made with Josh might be gone for good. He hadn't been like this before. Blaire remembered Caige telling her that every time he dropped his son off at school, Josh didn't want to go in, and he clung to his daddy. But he finally went in because he liked his teacher and remembered her.

This was different. He didn't know Blaire. She didn't want to believe any memory of her was gone. Sick with disappointment and desperate to make a connection, she did the only other thing that came instinctively and started to sing.

"Hi ho, hi ho—" she nudged his hand with the squirrel in time with the words "—it's off to work we go. Tra la la la la, tra la la la lo, hi ho, hi ho." She ended by poking his tummy gently with the squirrel's head.

Miraculously, he stirred and squeezed the tail with his free hand. She sang the song again, moving the squirrel clutched in his fingers in rhythm with the music. After several more renditions, his blue eyes looked at her and he smiled.

"Well, hi, big boy. I think you're awake." This time when she leaned down to kiss him, he gave three kisses back and kept tugging at her hand to play.

As they did a tug-of-war with the squirrel, Caige cupped the back of her head and pulled her close to him. A look of love radiated from his eyes, shining with such a luminescence it couldn't be mistaken for anything else. She felt it overflowing inside her before he kissed her fully on the mouth in front of his parents and half a dozen other family members who'd sneaked into the room. But she was too much in love to be embarrassed.

His uninhibited kiss was telling her so many things, she would have expired on the spot if it weren't for Josh, who was demanding attention from both of them.

"Later, darling," she whispered against Caige's hungry lips before she got to her feet on unsteady legs.

Reaching for his son's hand, she led him over to the

tree and sat down. He promptly sat next to her with the squirrel in one hand, his other one hugging her arm while she opened another present for him.

Caige joined them on the floor and kept giving her kisses on the neck and lips while his son sat enraptured with a new toy.

She handed the man she worshipped one of his presents, but he was too busy smothering her with kisses to open it. She did it for him and pulled it out of the tissue. There was an inscription on the trophy: Caige Dawson—World's Greatest Father.

"Blaire—" After examining it, he kissed her as if there was no tomorrow. This was joy to the world a hundredfold.

WHEN CAIGE STAYED WITH HIS folks, his son had to sleep in the same room with him or it didn't work, so there were two beds. Josh always needed a night-light.

Tonight Josh had been so wired, Caige hadn't put him down until after ten. He lay on one side of his son with Blaire on the other. It was very cozy on the twin bed. The more they were wedged together, the better Josh liked it. Once his head rested on the pillow, he fell into a deep sleep with the bunny and the squirrel clutched to him for dear life. In fact, they all slept for a while because of emotional exhaustion.

When Caige woke up again, he discovered Blaire studying him. He reached for her hand across Josh's body. In a minute the two of them would move to the king-size bed where Caige would like the arrangement even better.

"After I phoned you, I had to wait for you to call back. It gave me an inkling of how Commander Travis must have felt at the Battle of the Alamo when he called on the people of Texas to come to his aid. Unlike the tragedy that befell him and all those men, I saw my relief walk in the living room earlier today and knew I'd been saved."

"I'd been waiting for your call for days," she admitted. "If I'd had my way, I would have gone back to your house after we flew home from San Diego. This could have been avoided, but I understand the reasons why you made that decision. In a way, I'm not sorry about it because I had proof a little while ago that Josh really missed me. That's a very important thing to know if you're still going to let me be his caretaker."

He raised up. "We've got a lot of talking to do. Let's go over on my bed."

Her womanly smile seduced him. "Do you really think we'll get much of that done there?"

Caige stood up, careful not to disturb his son. "I don't know. Let's find out." He walked around the bed. After drawing her to her feet, he picked her up and carried her to the other bed. Once he'd laid her down, he didn't kiss her right away.

His avid gaze ate up her gorgeous features. "Do you know what time it is?"

"I haven't any idea, and I don't care," came her breathless answer.

"Ten after one. Merry Christmas, my love."

"Christmas? Oh, darling—"

"You called me darling. Do you know how long I've been waiting to hear those words from you?"

"Caige!" Her burst of exultation thrilled him. "You know I'm so in love with you, it's pathetic. After you left me at my parents, I was afraid I might never hear from you again."

He trailed kisses everywhere. "I was only trying to give you time."

"After five years, I didn't need any. I fell in love with you during our ride to the lab. Can't you tell I adore everything about you, including your son? The love you have for him, those pictures of him, it all tugged on my heartstrings." Her smile enchanted him. "I haven't been the same since."

He smoothed the hair from her temples. "You *are* going to marry me then?"

"For a brilliant Texas Ranger, that's probably the only unnecessary question you ever asked me."

"I still require an answer."

"Oh, you do, do you?" she teased. Soon they were tangled in each other's arms and she began kissing him with almost primitive hunger. This was better than any dream. A long time later she said, "I want to be married to you in every way possible. There's only one thing about you that's got me worried."

His dark brows furrowed, he lifted his mouth from hers. "What is it?"

"Are you really going to quit the Rangers?"

"I plan to do whatever it takes to make our marriage work."

She traced the lines of his mouth with her index finger. "You mean it?"

"Blaire, how could you even ask me that?"

"Then tell me the name of the person who's causing you to consider quitting. It couldn't be me because I didn't ask you to give it up. Josh didn't, either."

His thoughts reeled. "I'm doing it so I can be a better husband and father."

"How would doing that make you any better than you are? You already won the world's greatest father award."

"Be serious, darling," he begged.

"I've never been more serious in my life. Hold on. I'll be right back."

In the semidark, he watched Blaire roll away from him and hurry out of the bedroom. He never knew what she was going to do next. That's why he was so crazy in love with her.

She came back in under a minute with two gifts pressed to her chest. He watched in full-on curiosity as she opened one of them. In the box was another trophy. Blaire handed it to him. "Go ahead and read what it says."

He saw the writing: Ranger Caige Dawson—World's Greatest Texas Ranger.

"Here's one more present." She handed it to him. "You have to open this one yourself."

His throat had started to swell. He sat up and undid the wrapping. Inside the box was a smaller trophy.

"Read it out loud."

His eyelids prickled when he saw the words. "Josh Dawson—World's Greatest Junior Texas Ranger."

"Now, tell me, my love—how can Josh be a Junior Texas Ranger if his daddy quits? You're already famous, but I'd say thirty more years in the department will give you legendary status. Did I ever tell you I love the idea of being married to a legend? How about giving us another baby while you're at it? Someone who'll be as sweet and wonderful as Josh."

She was making him so happy it was scary.

"If you want to move here to be near your family, that's totally fine with me. But it'll be a longer commute to headquarters every day. I don't care where we live as long as you come home to me and Josh whenever you can.

"We know that doing Ranger work demands a lot from a good man, but someone has to do it, right? You're the best good man in Texas. I have the newspaper headlines from the other day to prove it. So...if you want to see a really big tantrum from me, try quitting."

Caige locked her in his arms, breathless with wanting her. "Have you finished?"

"I think so."

He burst into laughter. "You only think?"

"Well, I always like to leave a little wiggle room."

"In that case, let's talk about what's going to make *you* happy."

"That's the second most unnecessary question you ever asked me."

"Don't tease me about this, Blaire."

"I'm not. I'm planning to start playing the piano

again. When Josh is at school, I'll practice. Another joy I haven't been able to indulge in is gardening. He'll love helping me. You have a big yard. Perfect for what I'd like to do if you decide we're going to stay in Austin. Who knows? I might establish a nursery one day. The point is, you'll do your thing, I'll do mine and we'll make our dreams come true. What do you say?"

He took another long, deep kiss from her luscious mouth. "Maybe now is the time to bring up the subject of your Christmas present. Since it's settled that we're not leaving Austin, after all, I thought we'd find us some property and build ourselves a new house. But we'll go into the details another time because I have something else much more important on my mind."

Her cry of happiness reverberated in the bedroom.

Just as he thought the talking was over and the business of more fundamental communication was beginning, Josh showed up at the side of his bed clutching his pets.

"Well, hi, buddy."

"Oh—I woke you up, didn't I, sweetheart? Come here."

Caige chuckled as she helped his son climb on next to them. He kissed both of them.

"Welcome to my world, darling."

* * * * *

HEART & HOME

Heartwarming romances where love can
happen right when you least expect it.

COMING NEXT MONTH
AVAILABLE DECEMBER 6, 2011

#1381 BIG CITY COWBOY
American Romance's Men of the West
Julie Benson

#1382 A RODEO MAN'S PROMISE
Rodeo Rebels
Marin Thomas

#1383 A BABY IN HIS STOCKING
The Buckhorn Ranch
Laura Marie Altom

#1384 HER COWBOY'S CHRISTMAS WISH
Mustang Valley
Cathy McDavid

REQUEST YOUR FREE BOOKS!
2 FREE NOVELS PLUS 2 FREE GIFTS!

LOVE, HOME & HAPPINESS

YES! Please send me 2 FREE Harlequin® American Romance® novels and my 2 FREE gifts (gifts are worth about $10). After receiving them, if I don't wish to receive any more books, I can return the shipping statement marked "cancel." If I don't cancel, I will receive 4 brand-new novels every month and be billed just $4.49 per book in the U.S. or $5.24 per book in Canada. That's a saving of at least 14% off the cover price! It's quite a bargain! Shipping and handling is just 50¢ per book in the U.S. and 75¢ per book in Canada.* I understand that accepting the 2 free books and gifts places me under no obligation to buy anything. I can always return a shipment and cancel at any time. Even if I never buy another book, the two free books and gifts are mine to keep forever.

154/354 HDN FEP2

Name _____ (PLEASE PRINT)

Address _____ Apt. #

City _____ State/Prov. _____ Zip/Postal Code

Signature (if under 18, a parent or guardian must sign)

Mail to the **Reader Service:**
IN U.S.A.: P.O. Box 1867, Buffalo, NY 14240-1867
IN CANADA: P.O. Box 609, Fort Erie, Ontario L2A 5X3

Not valid for current subscribers to Harlequin American Romance books.

Want to try two free books from another line?
Call 1-800-873-8635 or visit www.ReaderService.com.

* Terms and prices subject to change without notice. Prices do not include applicable taxes. Sales tax applicable in N.Y. Canadian residents will be charged applicable taxes. Offer not valid in Quebec. This offer is limited to one order per household. All orders subject to credit approval. Credit or debit balances in a customer's account(s) may be offset by any other outstanding balance owed by or to the customer. Please allow 4 to 6 weeks for delivery. Offer available while quantities last.

Your Privacy—The Reader Service is committed to protecting your privacy. Our Privacy Policy is available online at www.ReaderService.com or upon request from the Reader Service.

We make a portion of our mailing list available to reputable third parties that offer products we believe may interest you. If you prefer that we not exchange your name with third parties, or if you wish to clarify or modify your communication preferences, please visit us at www.ReaderService.com/consumerchoice or write to us at Reader Service Preference Service, P.O. Box 9062, Buffalo, NY 14269. Include your complete name and address.

HARI1B

Lucy Flemming and Ross Mitchell shared a magical,
sexy Christmas weekend together six years ago.
This Christmas, history may repeat itself when they find
themselves stranded in a major snowstorm...
and alone at last.

Read on for a sneak peek from
IT HAPPENED ONE CHRISTMAS
by Leslie Kelly.

Available December 2011, only from Harlequin® Blaze™.

EYEING THE GRAY, THICK SKY through the expansive wall of windows, Lucy began to pack up her photography gear. The Christmas party was winding down, only a dozen or so people remaining on this floor, which had been transformed from cubicles and meeting rooms to a holiday funland. She smiled at those nearest to her, then, seeing the glances at her silly elf hat, she reached up to tug it off her head.

Before she could do it, however, she heard a voice. A deep, male voice—smooth and sexy, and so not Santa's.

"I appreciate you filling in on such short notice. I've heard you do a terrific job."

Lucy didn't turn around, letting her brain process what she was hearing. Her whole body had stiffened, the hairs on the back of her neck standing up, her skin tightening into tiny goose bumps. Because that voice sounded so familiar. *Impossibly* familiar.

It can't be.

"It sounds like the kids had a great time."

Unable to stop herself, Lucy began to turn around, wondering if her ears—and all her other senses—were deceiving her. After all, six years was a long time, the mind could play tricks. What were the odds that she'd bump into *him,* here? And today of all days. December 23.

Six years exactly. Was that really possible?

One look—and the accompanying frantic thudding of her heart—and she knew her ears and brain were working just fine. Because it was *him.*

"Oh, my God," he whispered, shocked, frozen, staring as thoroughly as she was. "Lucy?"

She nodded slowly, not taking her eyes off him, wondering why the years had made him even more attractive than ever. It didn't seem fair. Not when she'd spent the past six years thinking he must have started losing that thick, golden-brown hair, or added a spare tire to that trim, muscular form.

No.

The man was gorgeous. Truly, without-a-doubt, mouthwateringly handsome, every bit as hot as he'd been the first time she'd laid eyes on him. She'd been twenty-two, he one year older.

They'd shared an amazing holiday season.

And had never seen one another again.

Until now.

Find out what happens in
IT HAPPENED ONE CHRISTMAS
by Leslie Kelly.
Available December 2011, only from Harlequin® Blaze™